Entangled

By

Elizabeth Castle

Name: Castle, Elizabeth, author

Title: Unraveled

Description: Series: The Cantwell Quartet

Publisher: In The Air Publishing

Identifiers: ISBN 9781967731268 (ebook) | ISBN 9781967731275 (paperback) | ISBN 9798305405767 (amazon hardcover)

Cover Design by betibup33

Chapter One

Nash Camhion could no longer hear the words the federal agent was saying to him. His gray eyes darkened as his thoughts drifted back to the past. Twenty-seven years. It had been almost twenty-seven years, and the memories could still strike at any moment.

He remembered sweating in the confines of the dark room. In the shadows, every time he closed his eyes, he saw his grandfather being shot. Cormac Camhion had yelled his grandson's name as the man had grabbed Nash around the waist and tossed him in the utility van. All Nash could do was pray his grandfather was alive, that the blood pouring out of the wound wasn't fatal. But deep inside, he knew his beloved grandfather was dead.

Two men had grabbed him, but then there was only one. The one who had shot his grandfather remained. Thirteen-year-old Nash trembled in fear every time he heard movements outside the door, fearful he'd hear the man jingle his keys. He'd seen the padlock on the outside of the door that would lock him in.

On his first night, he had desperately tried to escape. The windowpanes were painted black, and barbed mesh wire kept him from the window lock. He'd tried punching through the wire to break the glass, but the sharp barbs cut his hands until blood smeared the glass and dripped on the floor. The glass had not broken. The man had come in and laughed at his attempt to escape. When the man grabbed him, Nash had fought as hard as he could. But after the sting of a needle, he had sagged in the man's arms. He'd been dumped on the four-poster bed that had been made up in the center of the room. He'd tied Nash's arms so that he couldn't claw or scratch him, but he'd been too weak, too tired from whatever had been in the needle to do more than whimper. His tormentor had tied his legs to the bed so tightly that he could barely move them.

The only light in the room came from a peeled paint spot at the top of the glass. The light glinted off the edge of the knife the man held. The man came to him the first time that night. Then a second. Then a third.

Nash bent over and tried to control his breathing, trying not to throw up the coffee he had drunk right before the federal agent had shown up at his door. He told himself over and over that the man couldn't hurt him. It was over. He wasn't a boy anymore. He knew how to defend himself. He could fight.

"Mr. Camhion? I realize this is a shock. And I know it can't be easy for you." Special Agent Donna Monaco held out her business card.

Nash ignored it as he got himself under control. He cleared his mind, let the feelings wash over him, through him, until they were no more. He took the card but tossed it on the coffee table. He took a good look at her. Her black hair was cut in a bob, and she looked more like a model than an agent. "I wish you would let it be. It's been twenty-seven years. MPD hasn't caught him. This case is so far buried at the bottom of the cold case files; I can't imagine why you are here."

Agent Monaco pursed her lips and continued. "As I was saying, there is new evidence. DNA from your crime scene was connected to a series of kidnappings and murders across the country. One of them was as recent as last year, right here in D.C."

Nash dropped down into the brown leather recliner. "But you don't know who the DNA belongs to? You said you have no suspects. So, forgive me, but who cares if my attacker's DNA is linked to other cases? You're no closer to finding this man than you were twenty-seven years ago."

The agent straightened her jacket and continued. "I'm going over each case, one by one. Trying to find what connects them other than DNA and MO. Your grandfather's murder is unique. No other family members were killed during the other abductions."

Nash cursed. "Two men, Agent Monaco. There were two. The one who shot my grandfather was the one who wanted me. The other man grabbed me while my grandfather was shot and then drove us to a building on the outskirts of the city. The man who killed my grandfather tortured me for three days. He got off on it, literally and figuratively."

The agent nodded. "The DNA from his semen. There was little in the case file outside of the investigation of the murder. My understanding is that your parents were adamant that your kidnapping remain hidden. It wasn't until quite recently that the DNA evidence came to light. Twenty-seven years ago, it wasn't processed."

Nash rose, his hands balled into fists as he began to pace. "My parents were trying to protect their traumatized thirteen-year-old son. But they didn't hide the evidence. If there was unprocessed DNA, then that is on the MPD."

The woman rose, her hand near her hip. "I'm not saying your parents covered anything up. I'm saying it's possible someone went to extra lengths to hide the kidnapping, including the evidence. What else do you remember?"

Nash put his hands where the agent could see them and forced his fists to unclench. "There is nothing else to tell. They wore masks. I was drugged. Then I was drugged again and again. My memories of the abduction are hazy. During my captivity, the man kept the room in the dark. I can say he was white. He had brown hair, was almost twice my height, and his breath smelled like peppermint and tobacco. There is nothing else. You have Gideon Eginhard's account from when he found me. His description was better than mine."

The agent opened her notepad. "Yes. It seems he's been investigating this case since he first became a police officer. The cold case detective gave me all the notes. My next stop will be to talk to him. You said your parents are out of town?"

Nash swallowed the bile in his throat. "Paris. It's their forty-fifth wedding anniversary. Paris was where they honeymooned. I don't want you to contact them. They weren't there. They didn't see anything. You already know who my grandfather was and who my parents are. Money seemed the logical motive. He got the money. He got away with murder. And he almost got away with killing me.

Leave them be. There's nothing they can tell you that I can't."

She nodded. "For now. I know almost everything I need to know about your family, Mr. Camhion. But as I said, your grandfather's murder is the unique piece. And I believe you were the first victim. If you think of anything else, please call. I'll keep you apprised if I find anything."

Nash had no faith that the agent would find anything. For one, she looked like she had just graduated from the academy. Second, DNA matches meant nothing without suspects. "I'll walk you out."

Nash opened the door and watched as the agent headed back to her nondescript car. The woman lifted a hand to someone in a car parked behind her. Angry, Nash stepped out onto the porch. Dusk was falling, the sun was setting, and he tried to let the cool air calm him.

A blonde woman climbed out of an old red Toyota Camry. Her hair was pulled up in a ponytail; she wore cheap department store slacks and an MPD windbreaker. "Hello, Ignatius."

That voice. The soft, smoky sound of his name on her lips stopped him in his tracks. The voice that helped him sleep at night. The voice he often dreamed about. "Freya."

She gave him a hint of a smile, but her hazel eyes were wary. "I'm sorry for showing up like this. I was hoping to beat Agent Monaco, but I got caught up in the lab."

Nash swallowed hard. They chatted almost every night, either by text or a call, but they had never met. The last two nights she'd opted to text, and they were brief. She had known the Feds were coming. He felt his temper flare. "I suppose I have you to blame for Agent Monaco showing up at my door. Dammit, I told Gideon to leave it alone."

Freya Jensen took a tentative step toward the porch. "Can I come in? I think we should talk privately."

Nash glared at her, but then shrugged. "Fine. Sure. Come on in. Just the way I imagined meeting you. Over the case of my dead grandfather."

Freya softly closed the front door as Nash left her to go to the kitchen. He heard her rubber-soled shoes following him. He started slamming cabinets, looking for where he had stashed the bottle of bourbon. He rarely drank, but it was that or punch a hole in his wall. He swore he could feel the man's breath on his skin. Could feel the knife as it sliced into his flesh.

Freya came and stood in the doorway. "Gideon did ask me to look into the files. But that was ages ago, and it was only about your grandfather's murder. I looked through all his records and evidence, and there wasn't anything else to find. I set it aside. There were active cases that needed me. But over the past few months that we've been talking, I've felt I needed to look again. I went rummaging through old evidence boxes. That's when I stumbled upon your name."

Nash filled the glass with the bottle of scotch he found. Bourbon or scotch; it hardly mattered. "So you stumbled onto the file of my kidnapping and assault."

Freya came to stand behind him. "Nash, I'm so sorry. I never thought I'd come across a file on you. But once I had…"

He took a large swallow. "Once you had, you just had to look."

Freya came around the counter so she could see his face. "I'm sorry."

He stopped and looked at her. Her brows, the same color as her hair, were furrowed. Her rosy pink lips, bare of lipstick or gloss, were pinched. Her cheeks were flushed, as was the exposed skin of her neck. Strictly speaking, she was average: average height, average weight, average looking. He would pass her on the street without taking a second look. But her voice, that smoky voice, brought his anger down a notch, and it was replaced with something else.

Nash finished the glass. "What's there to be sorry for? It's old news. Happened years ago. I'll tell you what I told Gideon. Leave it alone. My family has suffered enough. There is nothing you or anyone else can do to bring my grandfather back. You can't erase my memories. And bringing it back up over and over won't change it. DNA is not going to change it. If what Agent Monaco said is true, this guy has been all over the country for almost three decades, and the police and the Feds can't find him. Now get out of my house."

Freya unzipped her jacket. "I can help. Let me help."

Nash's eyes went to the white polo shirt with an MPD logo on the chest. Her waist was trim under the bulky jacket, and her shirt molded to her body as she took off her jacket. Lust was a sucker punch in the gut. Were she any other woman, he knew what would come next. But this was Freya, not one of the many women over the years whom he let catch him after they had chased him; one of the many women he'd used to erase the shame and humiliation his attacker left behind.

Nash set the glass down. "I don't want your help. I want you to leave."

Freya stood her ground, laying a hand on his bare arm. "Please, Nash. We're friends. You can trust me. I want to help."

Nash growled and grabbed her hips. He pulled her hard against his body. "You want to help me?"

Freya's eyes held his. They widened, but she didn't pull away. "Yes."

Nash's mouth crashed down on hers. He lifted her hips against his erection as his tongue invaded her mouth. She didn't fight him; she didn't push at him. Instead, she wrapped her arms around his neck. He lifted her thighs so they were wrapped around his waist, and he carried her to the back of the house. He broke off the intense kiss and dropped her on his bed. He fought for control.

"Nash?" Freya stayed where he had tossed her.

"One last time, Freya. You need to leave."

She lay on his bed, her lips swollen, her eyes darkened. She slowly shook her head.

Cursing himself and her, he stripped off all of his clothes. Naked, he yanked her to her feet and did the same to her. He pulled the polo off and barely gave a second glance at the sports bra she wore. He grabbed the fabric and yanked it over her head. Her bare breasts were tipped with tight pink nipples, and unable to resist, he bent his head and took the tip into his mouth. He sucked hard at her, and she whimpered in his arms. His hands went to the hook of her slacks, and he stripped both the pants and her underwear to her feet. More gently than the last time, he laid her back down so he could strip off her shoes and socks and get the pants off.

Freya's smoky voice called to him. "Nash."

Whatever was left of his control broke. He climbed over her and spread her thighs. His blinds were pulled, so he clicked on the lamp so he could see her. Her eyes held his. He bent and kissed her again, claiming her mouth again in a rough kiss. His hands stroked their way down her body, his roughened palms stopping at her breasts for a moment before his hands continued their journey. Her thighs fell away as his hands found her center. He stroked her, feeding her arousal until he was sure she could take him.

Knowing he should slow down, knowing he wasn't showing her an ounce of finesse, he settled between her thighs. Without another thought or hesitation, he plunged inside. He barely heard her cry out, was only peripherally aware as her nails dug into his back. His name on her lips was a breathy whisper in his ear.

He mindlessly surged into her, grasping her hips, desperately needing the softness of her flesh against his. It was only moments before he climaxed, surging one last time before collapsing on top of her.

Nash dropped his head against her hair, inhaling the soft scent of it. Then reality hit. He swore and climbed off her. She looked dazed as she lay there, her eyes not leaving his. He swore again. "I can't."

Nash went to the bathroom. The room was dark, but he didn't turn on the light. He went to the toilet, tossed the lid back, and vomited up the coffee and alcohol that were all that filled his stomach. He hung his head for a moment.

What had he done?

A soft knock came a few minutes later. "Nash. Come out. Please. We don't have to talk about it. We can just sleep."

Self-disgust assailed him. He'd used Freya like she was a nameless, faceless body. He would know; there had been many over the years. But Freya was his friend. At least she had been. He fought the unexpected and unaccustomed sting of tears as he got to his feet and brushed his teeth.

When he left the bathroom, Freya was under his sheets, and she had the comforter folded back. Her hair was still in a ponytail, though it was skewed. And despite what had happened, she was smiling at him. He stopped and took her in. She had the covers over her breasts, but he could see her bare shoulders were slim, as was her neck. Her cheeks and lips were flushed, and her slim hand lay on the bed. She patted the empty space beside her. Unable to resist, and not wanting to break whatever spell it was that she had over him, he slid under the covers.

Freya shifted until she was lying close enough to put her arm around him. He closed his eyes and drifted off.

* * *

Freya could hear the grandfather clock chiming the midnight hour from the living room. She had been lying next to Nash for hours. At some point in the night, he'd rolled until he was on his stomach, and he'd dropped into a deeper sleep. Knowing he would likely be that way for a while, she had drifted off.

But she was in an unfamiliar bed, and she was not accustomed to sharing, so she didn't sleep long. As she lay beside him, she thought back to the last man's bed she'd been in. Sadly, she distinctly remembered the last man's bed she'd been in, and it had been a long time ago. The interlude had ended in disappointment, physically speaking, much like this one had. And the next day, the relationship was over.

Freya watched Nash sleep. It might have ended the same, but she didn't want this relationship to end. There had been emotional satisfaction in being with him, holding him. She had seen the pain inside him and the need his eyes expressed. He had told her to leave. But she hadn't wanted to. When he'd come toward her, she knew what he wanted from her.

Nash Camhion. Women sighed and spoke about him in soft whispers. They all wondered what it would be like to have all that gorgeous masculine attention on them. Freya knew of his playboy image. And she wasn't immune. She had wondered what it would be like to have all of his attention on her. Now she knew. He had a broad, muscular chest and athletic body. And his, well, masculinity was not overrated.

She'd been in D.C. for over two years, but she knew who he was long before that. The Camhion family was well known in the city, but Nash had been her teenage crush. It wasn't hard to see the teenager he'd once been in the man that was lying beside her. She knew he had black hair. But now she knew it had a dark gray tone to it. She knew he had gray eyes. And now she knew how they darkened with desire.

He stirred and she laid a hand on his back. He settled at her touch. His hair was longer these days. During a press conference a few months ago, she had noticed. Now it was long enough to pull back in a ponytail. His skin was bronzed, and in the light from the lamp he'd left on, she could see some scars. Dozens of them in various lengths. She frowned as she touched one. Her stomach clenched. She knew a knife wound when she saw one, even one as old as these were.

She shifted out from under the covers. She knew he wouldn't appreciate her staring at him and speculating about them. When she'd followed him to the kitchen, she could see the demons inside taking hold. She had thought she could help him. She thought she could stop them from taking over. And she supposed she had. The moment his lips had taken hers, she'd been his.

She'd had plenty of fantasies, no doubt. She'd imagined a dozen ways Nash might make love to her. Tonight was something she couldn't imagine. His emotions were raw. His pain was on the surface. And every female bone in her body, every soft emotion she had inside, wanted to help ease the pain she saw. And because this was Nash, the man to whom she had spent many nights talking to and confiding in, she had given herself over to him.

She knew his best friend Gideon Eginhard because Gideon was a police detective where she worked as a forensic analyst. She'd helped Gideon on a case that involved his fiancée right after she joined the MPD. She'd later learned Penny was Nash's sister. A few months later,

Gideon had sought out her help involving another friend of his, Trenton Armstrong. She'd hunted down a crazy cult member and her serial killer son. She'd texted Nash a few times, but they were strictly work texts.

Then last year, Gideon had asked her to look into a woman who was trying to kill his friend Isaac Brandt. She'd been happy to help. She'd reached out to some old friends and had gotten her hands on a classified file of the woman Gideon was looking for. Nash had sent her dinner that night to thank her for helping. She'd texted him to say thank you, and they had messaged back and forth a few times.

She'd learned about Nash's grandfather when Gideon had asked her to look into the cold file on Cormac Camhion's murder. Gideon had given her only minimal details, but the files filled in the gaps. When Isaac's father was shot at Isaac's wedding, she had an urge to call Nash. Nash had been a witness to the shooting, and she imagined it triggered awful memories of his grandfather. She had sent him a friendly text, and for the past few months, they'd been texting and talking almost every night.

She teased him and called him Ignatius. She could lie in bed and think about him and think of him as not the playboy prince Nash, but Ignatius, her friend. She felt like she got to know a side of him he showed few others. He'd tease her, ask her what she was wearing as a joke, and they'd bid each other good night.

Fantasies were funny things, she mused. Nash was hers. She'd been falling in love over the phone, imagining what it might be like if they met. They would start off as friends, and then progress to something more.

It had only been a fantasy, of course. She didn't think Nash Camhion would date someone like her. He dated debutantes and models. During his modeling days, there had been any number of beauties on his arm. As far as she could tell, that hadn't changed much over the years. He admitted he wasn't seeing anyone; that Cantwell took up all his time. She could understand that. Her job took up all of hers. Of course, she wasn't a beauty, and men weren't falling all over her the way women did with him.

Freya slowly got dressed and was at a loss as to what to do. When she'd followed him into the kitchen, there had been so much pain in his eyes. And she was so sorry she had a hand in putting it there. She wanted to help. Sex wasn't what she had in mind when she'd shown up at his doorstep, but no part of her had wanted to say no. And she couldn't seem to strum up the regret she knew she should be feeling right now. Sex wasn't easy for her. She found it hard to get close to people. But some part of her felt like she knew Nash emotionally, as much as she now knew him physically.

She glanced as Nash's phone vibrated on his dresser. She saw Gideon's name. He wanted to talk about the FBI agent that had called him. She pretended to be Nash and sent a quick note saying he was exhausted and could they chat tomorrow. That seemed to satisfy Gideon, and he bade his friend good night.

Freya pulled on her black loafers and gave Nash one last look. No. She didn't want this to end.

Chapter Two

Nash made his way through the bullpen. Gideon said he'd be there the rest of the day. When Nash rolled out of bed this morning, he had gone to his phone. He saw a message back to Gideon he hadn't sent. The night had come slamming back. Freya had left sometime in the night. The part of him that was disgusted with himself was glad she had. He didn't want to face her. He didn't know what to say to her.

The other part of him wanted to go find her and apologize on his knees until she forgave him. He wasn't sure if he wanted to apologize for the sex, apologize for his lack of finesse, or apologize for being an insensitive bastard for using her the way he had. Probably all three, though he wasn't so sure he was sorry for the sex part. It had felt amazing to be buried inside her.

He was leaning toward the third option. Over the past few months, he had come to need her friendship in ways he had never needed another woman, not even Maggie. But right now, he wasn't sure he could look her in the eye for fear of what he would see.

So Nash had texted Gideon to ask when a good time would be to meet up. He'd poured a pot of coffee down his throat, taken a quick shower, and headed out. As he saw his reflection in the glass doors that opened into the bullpen, he realized he should have shaved. Nash was known for his impeccable grooming. Anytime he joined the ranks of normal men, as Trenton would say, the quartet worried that something was wrong.

He saw Gideon working at his desk, his face inches from his monitor. Gideon was at his most intense when he was working. Seeing that intense face, seeing the scars that were the legacy of Gideon saving him from a psycho killer, Nash thought back to the picture he had of the quartet on his dresser. He, Gideon, and Isaac were sixteen in the picture, Trenton fourteen. Even then, Gideon was the tallest. By the time they were sixteen, the scars on Gideon's face were just part of who he was, and seeing them couldn't dampen the pleasure of the day. Trenton had been telling some ridiculous story, while Isaac had shaken his head in disbelief. Gideon had put an arm around Nash, letting him know he wasn't alone. He loved all three men, but he and Gideon had a special bond.

Nash had always been the unspoken leader of the pack. He'd wanted to be strong for them. Gideon had looked to him to help him navigate life at the private school and to show him that there was life beyond the walls of poverty that Gideon lived. Isaac had needed him to pull him out of his shell, to reignite the spirit inside that his father had all but stifled. Trenton had needed the stability of an older brother, one to show him the ropes of how to navigate the real world outside of the confines of the cult he'd grown up in.

Gideon was the sword and the protector. When he'd gone into law enforcement, it had not come as a surprise.

He needed to right the wrongs. Trenton, the comedian, was practical underneath the comedic exterior. His amazing photography was a window into his soul. Despite all Trenton had been through, he saw the world as a place filled with beauty. Isaac was the brains; the one who made sure their schemes never got out of hand. He grounded them. He was the glue that held them together. Through the storms of their lives, Isaac could be counted on to bring reason to the chaos and carry them through until the storm subsided.

In reality, the picture should represent one of the worst days of his life. The night before the picture was taken, he'd hit his breaking point. It had been something so small. They were all spending the night at Gideon's house. The house only had two bedrooms, so Gideon slept in the living room, while his mom and sister Iris had the bedrooms. Mrs. Eldridge had been coming home late from work. He could hear the key turning in the lock; hear the jingle of her keys against her key ring. Bile had risen up in his throat, and he'd curled into a ball, fear making him break out in a sweat. Even though he saw her face as she quietly closed the door and went down the hall to her room, the fear had remained, memories surging that he couldn't control. He had desperately needed to get out.

Isaac was the first to follow him. Nash never knew how it happened, but Gideon and Trenton followed. Anger, grief, and fear all poured out of him. He wept as Gideon held him, Trenton and Isaac a circle of support around him. His friends had wept with him, absorbing his pain, listening to the painful secrets he kept pushed deep inside erupt out of him. Because of them, he made it through the night. He didn't break. He told them things he had never told another soul, not even to this day. They'd spent the rest of the night sitting on the front steps of Gideon's house. They'd watched the sun come up. That's where Nash's dad found them when he'd come to pick them up for a fishing trip. His dad had snapped the picture outside Gideon's house before packing them up and taking them to the lake.

He took a deep breath and went to Gideon's desk. "Hey."

Gideon looked up, his attention shifting focus. "Thanks for getting back to me. I had a phone call from an Agent Monaco. I didn't get the details yet, but her message said it was regarding you."

The darkness tried to rear up, but Nash thought back to Freya's face on his pillow as her arms came around him, and the darkness receded. "We'll need to talk in private first. And then we'll need to find Freya."

Gideon's eyes narrowed on Nash. "Why Freya? I haven't talked to her since we caught Avery."

Nash figured Freya hadn't said anything. Neither had he. "I was skeptical that Freya could find her. I still can't believe Isaac never told us a crazy woman was out to kill him."

Gideon grabbed his gun and badge from his desk, his tone pragmatic. "She'll never see the light of day. We can go to a room."

Gideon closed the door behind him. "So why is a federal agent wanting to talk to me about you, and how is Freya involved?"

Nash sat. He didn't want to talk about it, but with the Feds around, he didn't have a choice. "Special Agent Donna

Monaco showed up on my doorstep last evening. She wanted to talk about my grandfather's murder. She said DNA from my attacker has been linked to several other investigations across the country. One of them is right here in D.C. Kidnapping and murder of young teenage boys."

Gideon dropped into the chair across from him. "What DNA? There's no DNA. There were no fibers, no skin, no hair, or anything else at your grandfather's murder scene."

Nash's gaze dropped to the table. "The DNA that was taken off me."

Gideon's expletive was loud and clear in the room. "There was DNA collected at the hospital of that bastard? We've had it all this time?"

Nash's eyes found his. "The DNA doesn't match anyone in the databases. Just the other crimes. According to Agent Monaco, they don't have a suspect. But she said my kidnapping was likely the first, and that my grandfather's murder was unique. The other children were grabbed, cut up, and stabbed to death. The guy doesn't rape, but he gets off on the cutting and leaves plenty of DNA behind."

Gideon came and squatted down in front of his friend. His dark brown eyes held his, his dark hair framing his angular face. "Are you all right?"

Nash wanted to say yes, but he couldn't lie. "No. No, I'm not all right. I don't want the Feds poking into this. I told you I don't want to pursue this anymore. My parents are happy. My dad is finally retired. My mom and him are acting like newlyweds. You and Penny have been married for almost two years. I'm anxiously awaiting a niece or nephew. Both Trenton and Isaac got married and are ridiculously happy. The craziness of the past two years is over. I want to focus on Cantwell. I want to focus on the next steps for the business and the game's release. I don't want to keep rehashing my grandfather's murder or my kidnapping and assault."

Gideon took Nash's hand in his, his dark hair falling over his shoulders. "We want you to be happy, too. What about Freya?"

Nash shrugged his shoulders, a sure sign he was tense. "Freya and I have been texting and talking for a few months. She thanked me for dinner the night I sent over Italian, and we texted a little. Then she texted me after Isaac's dad was shot. We sort of fell into the habit. We talk at night sometimes when she's not working late."

Gideon rose and put his hands on his hips. "You and Freya? No kidding."

Nash bit his lip. "We're just friends. But because we've been talking, she started digging into my grandfather's murder again. She said she had looked into it for you but hadn't found anything new. But she got an urge to look again. While digging through the old boxes of evidence, she came across my name. She didn't tell me specifics yesterday, but my guess is she found the semen samples and ran them through the databases. She got a hit."

Gideon started pacing. "The Feds saw the match and contacted you."

"That's my best guess."

Gideon opened the door. "Freya should be in the lab. Let's go."

Nash reluctantly got to his feet. He wasn't comfortable

confronting her on her own turf, especially when she didn't know he was coming. But Gideon was now on the scent, and there was no calling him off.

Nash had never been in a forensic lab. The room was painted a drab gray, the floors were concrete, there was equipment pressed up against all the walls, and the surfaces of a dozen or so folding tables were covered in papers. The only clean spaces were the lab tables where evidence was processed. The room was filled with several people; most were wearing masks and gloves.

Gideon walked over to one of the lab tables. "Hi Freya. We need to chat."

Freya blinked behind her goggles but didn't stop what she was doing. "Go. I'll meet you outside. I need to finish this and then put it back."

Nash wasn't sure if he was happy she didn't notice him or offended. A night of sex and he wasn't a blip on her radar this morning.

Nash and Gideon went to the nearby break room.

Gideon poured them a couple of cups of coffee. "You look like you've already had your fair share, but here."

Nash took a sip and cringed. "Why is cop coffee so bad?"

Gideon shrugged and downed half. "It gets you through the day. Probably the machines are never cleaned. They're older than we are."

Nash laughed at the exaggeration, though probably not much of one. "Your fortieth is just around the corner."

Gideon's brow rose at that. "So is yours."

Nash got to his feet when Freya appeared in the doorway. His gaze held hers. Her lovely hazel eyes looked him over, and she seemed satisfied with whatever it was she saw. Then she blushed but got it under control.

Gideon turned. "Where did you find evidence on Nash's case?"

Freya's eyes sharpened, much as Nash would see Gideon's do when work took over.

"I've been working on an initiative to get old DNA processed. But mostly I was poking through the evidence and files on Cormac Camhion's murder. Behind the box, I found another one pushed all the way to the back. Then I saw Nash's name on it. The box was sealed."

Gideon growled. "And you wanted to see what was inside."

Freya came and took a seat. They were the only ones in the room. "You can imagine I was shocked to find unprocessed DNA. Swabs were taken at the hospital during the exam."

Freya turned apologetic eyes to Nash. "I didn't mean to snoop. I thought I'd find your clothes and maybe some duct tape or fiber samples. I didn't expect to find semen samples taken from your clothes and skin."

Nash struggled to keep control. He snapped at her. "I know where they were taken from."

Freya turned hurt eyes to Gideon. "Anyway, I ran the samples. Then I ran the profile. I ran it under an anonymous profile and was shocked when twelve hits came up. This guy is not worried about getting caught. So I called a friend of mine at the FBI. She said she'd discreetly look into it. Then she called me. She said she needed to talk to Nash."

Gideon pulled out a notepad. "I take it that was Agent Monaco."

Freya nodded. "Donna and I went to college together. We were in several of the same classes. She went on to the FBI Academy, and I went to the private sector. But we've been friends since, and we've worked together on a few cases over the years."

Gideon's pen was poised over the notepad. "No doubt she wanted the best."

Freya smiled at that. "Thanks for the vote of confidence. I have my own team, thanks to your recommendation."

Nash interrupted. "I knew I had you to thank for Agent Monaco landing on my doorstep. My parents covered up my kidnapping. I don't want this to make the local news. We've got too much riding on Cantwell's success to have this take over. There would be a media frenzy."

Freya's posture stiffened. "Agent Monaco knows how to be discreet. So do I. The FBI has no other leads. Yours is a fresh one. But like you said, there is no suspect. But Donna will take your file and compile it with the others. This guy is still active, and this is an ongoing investigation. But I don't see why your name, or the names of any of the other victims, would be disclosed. You have to remember, these are minors. And you were back then. Your identity, and theirs, is protected."

Gideon laid a hand over Nash's. "She's right. Even if it went to trial, the names would be kept undisclosed."

Nash felt some of the knot in his stomach unravel. But only a little. "I don't have anything new to share. I told Agent Monaco everything there is to know. We don't talk about this; we don't pursue this. And we damn well don't tell my parents. They obviously don't know there was DNA. They would have paid to rush it back then. As far as they are concerned, I was abducted, I was sliced up, and I was rescued. Got it?"

Freya could only nod. "Got it. I won't pry anymore."

Gideon shot his friend an odd look.

Freya rose. "I have to get back to work."

Gideon watched Nash watch her walk out. "Real smooth, Prince Nash."

Nash was beyond caring. He'd already screwed up with Freya. And yeah, any chance he had at fixing it, he'd screwed that up too.

Gideon finished his coffee. "What did you do?"

Nash swore and dropped his head in his hands. "I practically attacked her. She wouldn't leave. She wouldn't listen. She just stood there. And then I snapped."

Gideon laid a comforting hand on his shoulder. "I get it, man. I do. You might not have been raped by that sicko, but he messed you up."

Nash looked his friend in the eye. "I've lost track of how many women, Gideon. I used every one of them to try to eradicate the feel of that man's hands and knife on me. But it's still there. Twenty-seven years, and it sneaks up on me like it was yesterday. But I swear, I never meant to put Freya in that category. She was my friend. I was afraid to even meet her for fear I'd screw our friendship up. But she wouldn't leave. I told her to leave again, but she refused. And God help me, for a few moments, I forgot."

Gideon hugged him and then set him back. "I can't say I

know Freya well. But she's smart. Almost Isaac smart. I've seen her eyes when she walks through the station after a nasty case. She cares about what she does. There is a lot of compassion inside her. If you like her, I say figure out how to fix it. I've never heard you regret any of those women. But I saw how you were looking at her. I've seen that look in my own eyes. Trenton and Isaac, too."

Nash grumbled and crushed his cup. "I'm not in love with Freya. But I am sorry. Mostly."

Gideon tossed his cup. "I won't even ask what that means. I have to work with the woman. But come on. I want to look at your case file. You can either stay and we can talk about what Freya found. Or you can go home and work."

Nash thought about it. He scrubbed his hands over his face. "Let's go to your desk. You're going to look no matter what I say. And I'm not going to get anything done today. I'll text Lilah and she can handle the office. Trenton can keep her company. Ginny's working on a new project, so Trenton's feeling neglected."

Gideon snorted at that. "Yeah, right. Neglected. If anyone feels neglected, it's Penny. I've been working late a lot. Spring fever, I call it. All the crazies come out of hibernation."

Nash made a fake gagging sound. "I told you; I don't want to hear about your sex life with my sister."

Gideon hummed. "I wouldn't mind hearing a little more about this interlude with Freya when you stop feeling like an ass. She's cute. I like her. And something else occurs to me."

Nash was almost afraid to ask what it was, but he had to. "What?"

"A blonde. Long hair. Slim figure. Hiding in the mist?"

Nash cursed. "She is not the woman in your painting."

Gideon hummed again. "I have never been a believer in coincidence. Of course, I don't believe in precognition either. But you have to admit, I pegged three out of four."

Nash stomped off toward Gideon's desk. Gideon's paintings. They were the catalyst for three marriages. Nash would admit that Gideon's painting for his character was Penny. Isaac had written a fantasy novel about four men looking for women who would come to the men in their dreams, shrouded in mist. Four men, four brothers though not by blood, go on a quest to find the women. And in the spirit of fantasy, the men saved the women and lived happily ever after. Of course, after the dangerous mission to find them and save the world.

Gideon had read the book, but when Nash read it with the idea of turning it into a video game, Gideon reread it. That night Gideon couldn't sleep, and he'd done four portraits of how he imagined the women would look. One for each hero. Gideon's woman looked a lot like his sister Penny. Gideon had been in love with Penny since the day he'd laid eyes on her. Of course, Gideon fought it. And Penny needed to grow up first. Gideon had the dark looks of his Sioux great-grandfather, as did his character. His woman looked an awful lot like Nash's fair-haired sister. But it didn't take a genius to know Gideon had subconsciously drawn her for his character.

Trenton, the golden boy with his gold wavy hair and

tanned skin, believed his wife Ginny was the woman in his paining. The slender brunette with the slim hips and long hair did look a lot like Ginny. Though in contrast to the picture, Nash thought Ginny was shorter. But when Ginny had walked down the aisle of Trenton's boat to marry him, the dress she wore looked eerily like the one in the painting. And in her heels, she was a dead ringer.

Isaac, blond hair, blue eyes, neat and clean-cut, also didn't believe in precognition. But he'd fallen in love with Lilah, the woman Nash hired to do the graphic art for the game, and she looked like the redhead in the portrait. Her hair hung down her back in waves, and she had the fair skin the woman had. Nash was guilty of using the portrait as a way of pushing Isaac to finally do something about his desire for Lilah. Thank goodness he finally did. If anyone in the quartet deserved a loving wife and family, it was Isaac.

And sure, superficially Freya was a blonde. Her hair was a little bleached-looking, like she spent a lot of time outside. But Nash didn't want to get married. He didn't want the responsibility of a wife and family. He knew the evil that lurked in the shadows. Hell, broad daylight. Even thinking about a family of his own to protect made him queasy. But he could still hear his grandfather telling him one day he'd find the perfect woman, get married, and bring the next generation of Camhions into the world. His grandfather was old-fashioned, and the thought of a male heir, another generation to continue the legacy he started, made the old man's eyes glint with tears. Guilt would settle in when he thought of those tears and what Nash represented to him.

All Nash could think was that Cormac wasn't around to see what a disappointment Nash was to the family name.

But the way Nash figured it, babies were Penny's job. And now that she and Gideon had been married for a while, and with Gideon turning forty next month, Nash figured it wouldn't be much longer. And then there would be another generation of Camhions to fulfill his grandfather's legacy.

Gideon came up behind him. "Earth to Nash."

Nash's attention popped to the present. "Never mind. Forget it. No deal. I screwed up. Twice."

Gideon dropped into his chair. "Third time's the charm."

Nash mimicked Gideon's growl. "Open the file. Let's get this over with."

Gideon's eyes darkened as he read the file. "Nash, this is bad. Really bad."

Nash shoved Gideon out of the way when Gideon tried to block the screen. The smiling cherub face of a young teenager mocked him. Beside the smiling picture was a picture of the body as it had been found. The kid had been sliced up and stabbed once in the stomach.

"I can't do this." Nash practically fell out of his chair. "Freya said his DNA was tied to twelve more. That makes thirteen in total."

Gideon turned his screen and continued. "All teenage boys. All Caucasian. Same M.O. Cuts vary across the bodies, but the cuts all appear to be from the same knife. Cause of death was one stab wound to the abdomen. Same knife. There were only photos for wound comparison. No knives were found at the crime scenes. The FBI has been on this guy for twenty years. Most recent case was here in D.C.

last fall. Not even twelve months ago. Marcus Henney. Fourteen."

Nash came up behind Gideon. Thankfully there was no picture of the body on the screen. "He looks an awful lot like I did at that age."

Gideon pulled up the rest of the case file. "I noticed. A lot of them do. I'd say our guy has a type."

Peppermint and tobacco. The smell rushed him. Nash thought he was going to vomit again. Gideon saw and pushed his head between his knees. He could hear Gideon's voice talking softly to him, bringing him back to the present. He took several deep breaths until his heart rate came down.

Nash rose. "This has got to stop. I can't live like this. We can't let another boy die. Let's find the bastard, Gideon. And put this to bed."

Chapter Three

Freya swallowed the shot of Scandinavian aquavit. This was the only bar in town that stocked it. She'd have preferred a Norwegian brand, but beggars couldn't be choosers. One of these days she'd ask her uncle in Norway to send her a case.

Special Agent Donna Monaco sipped hers. She'd order it and then not drink it. "I don't know how you drink this."

Freya set her glass down, and the bartender poured her a second. "That's because you drink daiquiris and sweet wines."

Donna set her glass in front of Freya and asked for a strawberry margarita instead.

Freya sipped hers this time instead of tossing it back. "I stand corrected. Margaritas, not daiquiris."

Donna rested her chin on her elbow and contemplated her friend. "Your friend didn't take the news so well yesterday. He was pretty ticked off when I showed up. When I told him about the other murders, I thought he was going to pass out."

Freya shifted uncomfortably in her seat. "I knew he wouldn't appreciate me digging. I didn't know anything about his case until I found that box. Whoever covered up his kidnapping did a good job. Even Detective Eginhard, Gideon, didn't know there was DNA evidence. He knew of the file on the kidnapping, I'm sure, but he didn't mention it to me. What a mess."

Donna thanked the bartender and took a sip. "You really like this guy."

Freya thought the description weak. "Jeez, Donna, I'm more than halfway in love with the guy. Let's just say I had all sorts of fantasies about our first meeting. None of them involved me siccing a Fed on him and processing sensitive evidence that he obviously wants to stay hidden."

"You can do what I would do in this situation."

Freya swallowed the rest of her shot. "I don't think I'm going to like this."

"Jump his bones. Guys like him like a woman to take charge. And I carry a gun, which makes it sexier."

Freya hiccupped. "You don't even know him. And trust me when I say he's used to being the one in charge. An alpha male no matter which way you swing it."

"Okay, then. Assuming he swings it your way, let him seduce you. He'll go all caveman sexy and you'll be a lot less stressed when he's done."

Freya turned crimson.

"Oh my. You did. You go, girl."

Freya grabbed the third shot. Donna put her hand over the top. "Slow down. We've got all night. I want details."

Freya set the glass down. Donna was her best friend, and the need to share was overwhelming. "He did. Go caveman, I mean. He did. I didn't. And he fled the bedroom afterwards and threw up. It was not the romance of the century."

Donna slumped in her seat. "A guy who looks like that

and you didn't? Figures. But then, you seem to have that problem. Look at your last relationship. I'd say the fact that your friend fled instead of screwing your coworker is a step up."

Freya pushed the glass back, not feeling so well all of a sudden. "Thanks for the reminder."

Donna patted her shoulder. "Stephen was, what, five years ago?"

Freya's overly honest mouth opened. "Six."

Donna leaned her head on her shoulder, the margarita going straight to her head. "I'm sorry."

Freya couldn't help but laugh. "Thanks. Guys seem to be turned off by nerdy forensic analysts who spend more time at work and less time on them. And I think my job creeps them out. The rare occasions a guy asks me out, I end up canceling, and he stops calling. Last night was probably the last time I'll see him, unless you count today when he basically said he never wanted to see me again."

Both women agreed not to use his name in public. "Maybe Loverboy will surprise you. Other than the ending, how was it?"

Freya looked up at the water-stained ceiling. "It was exciting. He grabbed me like men do in the movies. I've never been kissed like that; like he hadn't kissed a woman in years and was making up for lost time. He looked just like he did when he was seventeen, all shiny and glistening on the cover. Better if you ask me. His chest was fantastic. The rest of him lived up to the promise of that glorious chest."

Donna slid further in her seat. "I am so jealous right

now. You got to see and touch him."

Freya kept her mouth shut this time. She'd barely touched him, except maybe to hold on. He had been moving so fast. He didn't give her time to think or react. Not that giving her time to think was likely to have made much of a difference. She was always so focused on the mechanics of it; afraid she'd do something wrong or embarrassing. Though when he'd touched her so intimately, she thought she might finally experience the real deal, if only he'd kept going. When he'd withdrawn his fingers, she had wanted to beg, but he had climbed between her legs, and it had been over before she knew it.

Freya hung her head. "No sense rehashing it. It happened. It was nice. It won't happen again."

Donna tried to stand. "You've spent months texting and chatting. That has to count for something."

Freya pulled out her wallet and set her card down for the bartender. "It says my love life is pathetic. I'm thirty-five, single, and I ruined the only prospect I've had in years."

"You only turned thirty-five last week. So you've still got five whole years until forty."

Freya helped Donna stand up. "Thanks. You're such a good friend. Let's get you home."

"Mmm. You can't drive. You've had two shots."

Not one to waste, she swallowed down the last shot. "Now that makes it three. I should sleep like a baby. Thank goodness neither of us works tomorrow. Let's get you home. Or you can stay the night at my house. We can get a greasy breakfast in the morning."

Donna giggled. "Too bad we're not attracted to each

other. It would save us a lot of hassle."

She made a drunken point, Freya supposed. "Come on, Grandpa Henry won't mind if you stay. He's got a guest bed with your name on it."

Thirty minutes later, Freya managed to get her tipsy friend to bed. It always amazed her how fast alcohol went to Donna's head. Three shots, and Freya was tipsy for sure, but she could still walk a straight line.

Freya popped her head into her grandpa's room before heading to bed. "Hi. I'm back. Donna is in the guest room."

Henry set his magazine aside. His accent was thick with his Norwegian upbringing. "Greasy breakfast tomorrow?"

Freya grinned. "Yep."

Henry patted the side of his bed, and she took a seat.

"How was work? You came home very late last night. And today you look sad."

Freya had told her grandpa about Nash. He'd heard her talking to him on the phone late at night. She hadn't gone into the details of what she was doing or what she had done. As far as Henry knew, Nash was a friend she'd met through a colleague at work. Which was the truth, if a bit of a stretch. But she couldn't tell him what had happened between them, and she was too tired to come up with a half-truth that would satisfy his curiosity.

So she used the excuse she always used. It was the truth, after all. "Yeah, work's been hard. Caught a bad case. Kids. It never gets easier."

Henry patted her cheek. "You're a sweet girl. It will never get easy for you. But I am proud of you."

She kissed his cheek. "Thanks, Grandpa. I'm going to go

to bed."

"How many shots did you have? I can smell it on your breath."

Freya gave him a facetious smile. "Three."

Henry patted her cheek again. "That's my girl. Now off to bed."

She waved and went to her room. She stripped off her clothes and tossed them in the laundry. The black slacks were wrinkled from a day spent in them, her shirt a little musty from sweating under the radiation suit she'd had to wear today. With a wrinkle of her nose, she tossed her sports bra and underwear onto the pile. She glanced over at herself in the mirror. She thought she looked pretty good. Her breasts were a nice size, not too big or small. Her waist was trim, though there was always a little pooch to her belly. Her thighs were a little rounded, but overall she was toned from the bike and treadmill she used at the gym.

Freya closed her eyes. Nash. Had he liked what he had seen? Had he even looked?

Annoyed with herself, she grabbed a nightshirt and tugged it on, this one with rainbows all over it. She set her phone on the nightstand in case work called and settled under the covers.

Shortly before midnight, her phone buzzed. She rolled over and grabbed it. Her heartbeat sped up.

The message was from Nash. *We didn't get to talk about last night. I just wanted to say I'm sorry.*

Freya's hand squeezed the phone. Of course, he was sorry. He hadn't even wanted to meet her, and she'd forced her way into his life. She'd caught him at a vulnerable moment, and she'd taken advantage of the situation. He had told her to leave. But she hadn't wanted to. She had wanted to help him. Perhaps not necessarily with sex, but she'd been fantasizing about it enough, and when he'd grabbed her and kissed her, she had no resistance. He was probably angry he'd taken her to bed. Because he was definitely angry with her that she'd brought a federal agent to his door.

She rolled onto her side, deciding if she should reply or not. But it didn't feel right not to. *I understand. Good night, Ignatius.*

The phone remained silent. She felt tears sting her eyes, but she wasn't going to cry. It wasn't her first failed relationship, but she could at least hope it was the last. Though her track record said otherwise. Maybe she'd try to date again in six years.

She tugged the blanket to her chin and willed herself to sleep.

* * *

The entire team, except Gideon, was working hard as they got into the final stretch before the game launched. Nash was overdoing it on coffee again, but he was exhausted and running on nothing but coffee and adrenaline. He wanted the launch to be perfect. He'd opted to go with his own platform instead of selling the game to a larger company to host it. This game was his, and no matter what happened, he wanted to keep full control of it and its future.

Cantwell's office took up the second floor of his house. He'd purchased the house across the street from his sister, Penny. She'd been horrified he was going to live so close, but she couldn't sway him. He loved the house. The ground floor was all the room he needed. It had a large master suite on both floors, a second smaller bedroom, as well as a second bath, a full eat-in kitchen, and a massive living room. He had converted the three large bedrooms upstairs into Cantwell's offices.

But the thought of his bed right below him made him think about last night. He hadn't been able to sleep. He swore he could smell Freya's scent on his sheets. He'd tossed all night, trying to sleep. He had an early morning, so he'd gone to bed early, but sleep eluded him. Normally he'd text Freya. She'd answer him, and they'd text or chat for a few. The conversation would lull him until sleep came.

But after what happened, it didn't seem right to text her to help him sleep. He'd been rude. He'd been curt. And he could tell he'd hurt her feelings. He didn't know her facial expressions yet, but that one was hard to miss. So with a mixture of lust and guilt, he'd sent her an apology text. Her response might have been short, but the fact that she called him Ignatius and not Nash had lightened his mood. Perhaps he hadn't completely screwed up after all.

And then what, he thought? Did they pick up where they left off? Did they try to go back to the way things were? Neither sounded like an option.

Penny tapped him on the shoulder. "Hey. You're drifting again."

Nash turned to his sister. Her blonde bangs framed a

pixie face. It was hard to see any family resemblance between them, despite having the same parents. She was six years younger than he was, and they had always been close. He hated it when she worried about him, like he could tell she was doing now.

Nash pulled over a chair. "What's up?"

Penny tucked her hands between her knees as she sat. "I stopped by the police department yesterday to see Gideon. I wanted to surprise him with lunch. I saw what he was working on. Were you going to tell me Gideon was working on your case?"

"He's always working on my case."

Penny slowly shook her head. "Not like this. Were you going to tell me?"

Nash tossed his pen down. "I don't know. I don't want Mom and Dad to know. There is no reason to drag them into this when nothing will come of it."

Penny leaned closer. "You don't know that, Nash. What if this is it?"

Nash struggled to keep a hold on his temper. "All right. Let me give you the cliff notes version. Freya was poking into Grandfather's case. While doing that, she came across an evidence box. It had my name on it. She opened it and found twenty-seven-year-old DNA. It was preserved enough that she got a profile. The profile matched the DNA taken from a recent kidnapping. She turned my file over to a friend of hers who is in the FBI and has been investigating the attack. Needless to say, I was not happy when an FBI agent showed up on my doorstep. But the FBI has been looking for this guy for twenty years. They don't have a suspect to match their DNA to. So there is no point in getting anyone's hopes up that the police or the FBI are any closer to catching this man because the DNA in my case matched the DNA in theirs."

Penny's mouth dropped open. "What DNA? The police have had DNA from your attacker, and they never ran it?"

Nash found he could smile. "You sound like Gideon. I'm going to be honest, Penny, I don't remember a lot of what went on at the hospital. I remember Mom and Dad crying a lot. I remember doctors and nurses coming and going. Eventually a lot of cops showed up with a child psychologist and asked me all sorts of questions. Which at the time I refused to answer. They probably collected all sorts of evidence, from the duct tape to the clothes I wore, and who knows what else."

Penny wiped a stray tear. "You didn't talk for a week. Grandmother took me back with her to Baltimore after the funeral. With Grandfather dead, and you unable to tell the police any details of the killer, Dad thought it best I go with her. I was so scared."

Nash took her fingers in his hand. "It was scary for everyone. Gideon got a much better look at the man than I ever did. The man kept the room dark. Gideon didn't draw blood, so there was no blood DNA on him. The only blood found on him was his own from the gashes on his face. I'm sure his clothes were taken into custody since he physically fought with the man, but nothing came back that Gideon's aware of. It's too hard to say all these years later how a DNA sample was missed from the evidence taken at the hospital. But all it tells us is that I wasn't this man's last victim."

Penny turned her fingers in his so she could hold his hand. "What about Freya? Maybe she can help. If she's the one who found the DNA and the connection, maybe she could help find this guy."

Trust Penny to hit on the heart of his current dilemma and not know it. "Freya was doing her job when she found the connection. Penny, it's been too long. Gideon hasn't found him. The MPD hasn't found him. And now we've learned the FBI hasn't found him. I doubt one forensic analyst is going to make much difference."

Penny's shoulders dropped. "I suppose. I guess it was too much to hope that the FBI would know who the DNA belongs to."

Nash squeezed her hand and let it go. "Puzzle pieces, as Gideon would say. So my story is part of a bigger picture than we realized. But that doesn't get us any closer."

"Guess not. And I agree. It's best not to tell Mom and Dad. Grandmother, either. She'll be ninety-two in a couple of months. I don't know if her heart can take it. She says she's come to peace with it. She just waits for the day she'll see him again."

Nash wished he could say the same. He'd spent the last few years wishing it would all go away. What difference did it make if his grandfather's killer was found? It wasn't until Freya ran that DNA that Nash knew this man was even alive. Twenty-seven years was a long time; part of him hoped that he'd met an untimely demise and was gone. Learning the man was very much alive and still terrorizing and murdering children was horrifying. He'd meant what he said; they needed to catch this guy. Not for him, but for the other boys. But Nash had no idea how.

Isaac came over. He adjusted his tinted lenses that covered his damaged eye. He'd saved Trenton's life, but the burn scars and permanent damage to his right eye were reminders of how close they had come to losing Trenton and Isaac.

"Everything all right?"

Penny stood. "Everything is fine. I'm just worried about Nash. He's had enough caffeine to power a small village."

"It would be an interesting solution to our energy crisis."

Nash groaned. "Trust you to take that seriously. Where's Delilah?"

Penny nudged Isaac with her elbow. "Yeah, Isaac, where's Lilah? I saw you two sneaking off earlier."

Isaac crossed his arms over his chest. "And who did I catch just two days ago sneaking off with Gideon when he was supposed to be working?"

Penny raised her hands. "I plead the fifth. And since I don't have a vested interest in Cantwell, I'm going to go home. I've got some contracts I need to go over before Monday. Gideon swears he's taking tomorrow off. I can't remember the last Sunday we got to spend together."

Nash filed away that bit of information.

Trenton swung past the desk and stopped. "Hey, you can't have a party without me."

Penny bumped Trenton's hip with hers. They'd been friends a long time. "I was just catching up with Nash. Isaac poked his nose in."

Trenton bit his lip. "It is pretty big. It's hard for him not to."

Isaac shoved his hand in Trenton's face. "Yeah, yeah. We've heard that one a dozen times."

Trenton followed him. "And it's still funny. You just have no sense of humor."

Penny shook her head at their retreating backs. "I don't know how you guys get any work done. But I really do need to go over those contracts. There is a piece of real estate I'm thinking of investing in. You'll keep me up to date, won't you? He was my grandfather, too. And I love you, Nash. The memories of those days when you weren't with us still haunt us as much as they do you."

Nash rose and hugged her. "I promise."

Satisfied, Penny left.

Nash stretched his shoulders and turned back to his computer. He had left out a lot of details, and he knew it. He'd been protecting her from what had happened for years. To this day, she only knew minimal details. And he trusted Gideon wouldn't tell her any more than she already knew for the same reasons he didn't. Gideon would want to protect her and shield her from the ugliness in the world.

Nash picked up his cell phone and tapped it. What difference could one forensic analyst make? Guess he wouldn't know unless she tried. And deep in his gut, he had a feeling Freya could make all the difference.

Chapter Four

Nash waited at the reception desk for Freya. He'd been tempted to text her again last night, but he'd decided that showing up unexpectedly might throw her off balance. And if off balance, it might be easier to convince her to help him, despite the way he had treated her.

He saw her come around the corner and his breath caught for a moment. She looked very much like she had the day he first saw her. Her hair was in a ponytail, her shirt and jacket were still emblazoned with the MPD logo, and her slacks were still ill fitting. But for a moment he had seen her as she'd been the other night: her face inches from his, her naked body under him.

Her hazel eyes caught his as she came around the desk. "Well, Nash, I wasn't expecting you to show up again."

"Can we talk? It's lunchtime; I was hoping you could slip out."

He didn't like the way she looked at him, as if she were trying to see inside. She made him want to shuffle his feet like an awkward teenager.

"All right. Let me get my bag and jacket."

He let out the pent-up breath he didn't realize he'd been holding. The receptionist smiled at him, one that said I'm available. He gave her a slight smile back but turned away from her. A few minutes later, Freya came back.

Nash tucked his hands in his trouser pockets to keep his hands off her in even the most casual way. "How about we walk for a bit?"

Freya stepped out into the sunshine and pulled out a pair of sunglasses. "So what do you want to talk about? I'm open to discussing only one topic."

Nash rolled his shoulders. "Do I get to choose which one?"

Freya shook her head. "No."

Nash glanced at her. The sunglasses shielded her eyes. His pace slowed. "I saw the pictures."

Freya missed a step and stopped. "Oh, Nash. Why?"

"I had to see."

She turned and they headed toward a nearby park. "I guess I can understand that. When I saw the evidence box, I had to look."

"I suppose it's the same thing that drives Gideon. But unlike Gideon, I can't change the outcome. But I can help you and Gideon change it."

Freya spoke after they passed a young couple. "You told me to leave it alone."

Nash swung in front of her and forced her to a stop. His gray eyes were the color of storm clouds. "Why am I alive? Why am I alive and those other children are not? What kind of man tortures and murders kids?"

"That doesn't sound like a rhetorical question."

Nash ran a frustrated hand through his hair, trying to find the right words. "I survived what those other boys didn't. Why didn't he stab me in the gut and leave me to die? Why was he attempting to move me from where he'd held me for three days?"

Freya took a step back. "If you were the first, he may have learned his lesson. You were the one who got away, and he wasn't going to make that same mistake again."

Nash growled. "It can't be that simple."

Freya looped her arm through his and tugged him to follow. "Perhaps not. Donna thinks there was something special about you. Maybe your grandfather. Think about the timeline. The second man already had you at the van when the first man shot him. He didn't have to shoot your grandfather. Yet he did. The second man tossed you in and drove the getaway vehicle, but you never saw him again. Only the murderer."

"Agent Monaco said my grandfather's murder is what sets my kidnapping apart from the others."

"Yes."

Nash led them over to a bench away from the walkers. "The question I keep asking myself is where was he taking me?"

Freya folded her hands on her lap. "That's probably the same question Gideon has asked himself dozens of times. Was it his accomplice? Was it someone who orchestrated the kidnapping? Did the guy have some fantasy of where to kill and dump you?"

All questions he'd asked himself. "He never came back. He never tried to grab me again. My parents had around-the-clock protection everywhere I went. So did he give up, or did he never try?"

Freya slipped her glasses off. "What do you want from me, Nash?"

"Do what you did to find Trenton's stalker. You took DNA and matched it to a relative of his. Maybe you don't have this guy on file, but maybe you have someone he's related to."

Freya reluctantly shook her head. "I got lucky. I found Luke Connor through genealogy websites. The only reason there was anything to match was because his mother was obsessed with genealogy, and so were many of the cult members who were trying to reconnect."

"But you could get lucky again, right?" Nash wasn't going to drop it.

Freya sighed. "Anything is possible, I suppose. But we're talking about what could amount to months of work and no results. And the results are not full proof. And I'd have to get permission to spend my time and resources on it."

"Wouldn't the FBI want to try? Or couldn't you run it on your own time? Or I can pay for it."

Freya took his hand. "It's not just money, Nash. It's not just a matter of running a profile through a database, though it is part of it. We can predict genetic factors and we could generate some leads. We can use the DNA to try and recreate a potential family tree to find possible suspects. But they could all be dead ends."

Nash squeezed her hand. "What about the Golden State Killer case? DNA was used to create a family tree that led to his arrest and conviction."

Freya conceded. "All right. I'll see if I can get authorization to work on it. I can't just take evidence and run it on my own outside of my job. Anything found we want to be able to use in court. There are legal channels that have to be followed."

He lifted her hand and kissed her knuckles. "Thank you, Freya."

They sat on the bench, but Nash was at a loss for words. "Why don't we get lunch?"

"We'll need to make it quick."

Grateful she didn't insist on going back to the station, they headed toward some nearby food trucks. He took their order and found a table for them. When he brought the food back, Freya had her glasses on again.

Nash ate some of his lunch while Freya finished most of hers. "I've missed talking to you."

Freya set her napkin down. "I've missed talking to you. But things can't go back to the way they were."

Nash pushed his food aside. "But they can move forward."

Freya hesitated before speaking. "Forward how?"

"We could go out to dinner. We could see a movie. Anything you want."

Freya stood. "I don't know."

Nash came to stand next to her. "I know you're mad at me. And I know I was a jerk. I can't undo what happened. I've been trying to figure out what to do about you and me. The only thing I know is that I don't want to walk away."

Freya started to lift a hand to his face but then stopped. "And you're going to just pretend we didn't have sex?"

Nash took a step closer. "No. I don't plan to pretend we didn't go to bed together. Frankly, I don't want to forget. I'd love to do it again. But I rushed things, and I know it. I used you, and I don't know how to make it up to you."

Freya didn't pretend to misunderstand. "I didn't feel used. I could have left at any time. But I'll agree you rushed things. And I need time to think."

Nash took a step closer. He pulled her sunglasses off. Her hazel eyes were wary. He wanted to kiss her but knew that wasn't what she wanted. "Can I call you?"

Freya took the glasses from him. "You can text me. We'll go from there."

Nash cleaned up their mess and walked her back to the station. He stayed outside. "You'll let me know what your boss says?"

"I'll run it past Donna first. It's an open federal investigation. But local law enforcement is allowed to help. Your grandfather's case is a cold case. There are other open cases, but they fall under federal jurisdiction."

Nash tucked his hands in his pockets again. "Thank you, Freya."

She stopped at the double doors. She kept her back to him. "You're welcome, Ignatius."

That made him grin. He went back to where his driver was waiting. "Back to Cantwell."

The older man nodded. "Yes, sir."

* * *

Freya went back to her lab. She picked up the phone. "Agent Monaco."

"Hi, Donna, it's me. Nash did a one-eighty."

"Well, well. Business or pleasure?"

Freya looked at her knuckles where Nash had kissed

them. She grabbed a DNA swab and swabbed her skin. She didn't have Nash's DNA on file, but no doubt his profile would be the other profile in the DNA sample she'd processed from Nash's evidence kit. But it was best to be thorough if it went to trial.

She tucked the phone to her ear. "A little of both. He's wondering if forensic genealogy could help track our killer."

Donna's hum came over the line. "Anything's possible. I've not had a case where we've used the technique before, but I know you have. Feeling up to processing a few million records?"

Freya stared at the swab. "This guy is bad news, and we both know it. He's killed at least twelve boys in twenty-seven years. That number will only grow if he's not caught."

"Solving the murder of Cormac Camhion would make my superiors happy. D.C. is all about politics, and the Camhion family has a lot of influence. Likely to make a few politicos happy."

Freya replied. "The opposite, too. I can't help but wonder why that DNA was never processed. Detective Eginhard knew nothing about it. Nash admits he didn't either. If his parents are loving parents, and current evidence says they are, would they have had it suppressed? And who would have been willing to suppress it?"

Donna's phone beeped. "I'm going to let you find the answers to those questions. I've no doubt you will. I'll take this back to my boss, and we'll go from there. Chat you up later."

Freya tucked her phone in her desk. She picked up the swab. What other evidence wasn't processed, she wondered. Could there be other evidence? Other cases?

The lab was quiet, so she took a seat at her desk and started digging into the different case files handled twenty-seven years ago. Four hours later, she had a list of cases to start with. The older files were in storage, but the computer gave her bare facts, and she found several cases that were of interest. It made her heart hurt to see so many old files filled with crimes against children.

Gideon poked his head into her office. "I just got a call from Captain Barnes. He assigned me to the murder of Marcus Henney. His case file is the one Nash saw. Marcus's murder might be tied to a federal case, but it's a local murder. I've already dug into Cormac Camhion's case, and the Cold Case detective is happy to turn it over to me. FBI is requesting your help, and I'm not stepping out."

Freya printed out a copy. "Donna can be very persuasive. I've already been digging into some old cases. I wanted to see if there are any cases that might be linked or have similar victims."

Gideon took the printout. "Any of these promising?"

Freya folded her arms across her chest. "You know as well as I do that the likelihood of any of the old cases being related is negligible."

Gideon read the names. "Leg work. That will be how this case is solved."

Freya shrugged. "I figured I'd burn it at both ends. I'll pull any recent cases that could at all be similar to Marcus Henney's murder. The list you have is of cases over twenty years old."

Gideon handed her back the list. "I'm going to go

through the FBI files. See if there are any other patterns or leads."

Freya nodded. "I've got cases backed up. But I'll get started on this. I also have Nash's DNA to run. And I want to see the evidence in Marcus's case."

Gideon started to turn but then stopped. "What about Nash?"

Freya watched Gideon's face go from focused and intense to concerned. She tucked her hands in her pockets. "I don't know."

Gideon's brow furrowed. "He's my best friend. He's gone through a lot. Still does. It's none of my business, but he likes you."

Freya felt her face flush. "I suppose he told you."

Gideon shrugged. "No details. But he is sorry for the way he acted, if that helps."

"So he said."

Gideon left it at that. "Keep me posted. I'll do the same. Let's find this guy."

Freya watched him leave. He was a very intense man, and a bit scary, if she were honest. He towered over almost everyone in the precinct. His black hair had a wave, and his eyes were almost black. The scars that crisscrossed his right eye added to the impact he had on people. But she had seen care and compassion in his eyes when he spoke of his friend.

Freya stretched the kinks out of her shoulders and set the case list in her inbox. She had other cases pending, and she wanted to work on those so she could focus on Nash's, Cormac's, and Marcus's cases. But she wanted to go back to the evidence room and take a second turn.

Ignoring the time, she headed to the evidence room. The room was meticulously ordered even though it looked a little chaotic. She was making it her mission to go through all the old files and to process the backlog of DNA samples. When cases were solved quickly, additional evidence was not always processed. But Freya believed that the old samples needed to be processed and logged. She also worked with the Cold Case department. Some of the cases would never be solved, but like with Nash's case, links could be made. New or old, everyone deserved justice.

Freya sorted through the files. She was startled when the door opened. She relaxed when she saw Captain Barnes. "I take it you're looking for me."

The captain eyed the rows and rows of boxes. "Of all the rooms in this building, this one is the most depressing and the most hopeful."

Freya's gaze went to the shelves of evidence. "Sir?"

"So much proof of what people do to other people. And yet in these boxes is the hope the victims and families rely on. The hope that in one of them is that one piece of evidence needed to solve their case."

Freya waited for him to get to his point. He usually wasn't one for small talk.

Barnes's sharp gaze went back to Freya. "The murder of Cormac Camhion was one of those cases that brought a lot of attention to the D.C. police. Reporters speculated about who killed him, and there were dozens of leads we chased. I was a rookie then, but we were all talking about it. Today if a murder is committed in broad daylight, there are dozens of videos and pictures of it. That was good work finding that DNA sample."

Freya shifted uncomfortably. "I know I should have asked permission to run it. But I had been authorized to help Detective Eginhard on Mr. Camhion's murder."

"But a kidnapping is a whole other story. Until I became captain, I didn't even know about it. The kidnapping had been kept out of the press, and I don't remember hearing even rumors."

Freya figured she was already in deep, so she asked, "Who might have been in a position to suppress evidence?"

Sharp blue eyes turned her way. "Suppress?"

She cleared her throat. "Twenty-seven years ago, evidence was collected. It would have gone through the evidence chain from the hospital to the police station. Evidence from the murder was processed, but a DNA sample was lost, and the case file I found on Nash Camhion was bare bones. The detective in charge documented very little."

Barnes considered that. "Most of the case revolved around the murder. If the kidnapping was handled discreetly, maybe the detective felt that all the evidence tied back to the murder."

"And yet there was DNA that tied only to Nash Camhion's kidnapping that was never processed. Forgive me, sir, but it's inexcusable."

Barnes turned his gaze to the ceiling. "Detective Elliot Dashevsky was in charge of that case, if I remember correctly. Arrogant S.O.B. He bragged about how he was going to solve the crime of the year. He wanted glory.

Worst kind of cop in my opinion. Doubtful he'd cooperate with the investigation, especially if you attack his handling of the investigation."

She mentally filed the name. He would be one of the people she investigated. But the captain was right; it was unlikely Detective Dashevsky would be cooperative. And he would likely be retired by now.

The captain continued. "Anyway, the Burton case is priority. The case is airtight, but we need those samples processed so we can turn it all over to the D.A. The rest of your cases you can pass to your team. I don't suppose I have to tell you to be discreet while investigating this case."

No doubt he gave Gideon the same lecture, she thought. "No, sir."

"Good. Now go home. It's late."

Freya glanced at her watch. It was already nine o'clock. She followed the captain out and went back to her lab. She checked her phone. No missed texts. Feeling deflated, she fetched her stuff and drove home.

Her grandpa was already in bed when she got home. Tired, she stripped and dropped into bed. She had just turned off the light when her phone buzzed.

Her heart racing a little, she picked it up.

Hope you got home safe. Gideon said he saw you leaving work not that long ago.

She hadn't even noticed the detective at his desk. *Just turned in for the night. Did work go well? Cantwell launches any day.*

His reply was brief. *Twenty days and counting.*

She snuggled under the covers. *We're both going to be very busy the next few weeks.*

She could hear his tone through the text. He was annoyed. *Going to use that as an excuse to avoid me?*

It was as good as any. *Yes. Good night, Ignatius. Sleep well. Good night, Freya. Text you tomorrow.*

She set the phone on her nightstand and rolled onto her side. How she wished she were there with him right now. But they had rushed things, and she knew she needed to be sure of what she wanted before agreeing to see him, even if it was just dinner or a movie. Nash was open to an affair, and though she forgave him, it had hurt when he'd turned on her the next day. Not that he didn't have good reason.

But now she was the woman investigating his grandfather's murder and his kidnapping. She was probably only one of a small handful of people who knew what had happened to him when he was thirteen. She had seen the physical scars. And that night in his bed, she had seen his emotional ones, too. She wasn't afraid of him; she was afraid she'd hurt him. Could he separate her job from the woman? The few men she dated couldn't. And with Nash, she was intimately involved in his case. She could imagine what she would feel if she kept deep secrets inside her, and the man she was involved with knew them as intimately as she knew his.

She flipped over, bringing her knees to her chest. No, she should keep her distance from Nash. She should focus on his case and do what she could to find the man who had done this to him, his family, and that of a dozen other families.

But she didn't know how she was going to ignore the man she was in love with.

Chapter Five

The next two and a half weeks were chaotic. He couldn't believe the launch of Cantwell was already here. Nash paced the conference room after having been up all night. Early reviews were trickling in. Gaming sites were buzzing. Critics were raving. He took the first deep breath he'd taken in three years. All the hard work had paid off.

Isaac's book that the game was based on also launched. Gaming, fantasy, and romance fans alike rushed out to buy their copies. Thousands of digital copies had already been sold in the past few hours. Isaac was fielding dozens of calls from his agent. Nash knew Isaac was pleased that the book was getting as much attention as the game. He had an extensive fan base, and those fans were raving about his departure from his usual sci-fi books.

Gideon came back with a bottle of champagne, Lilah following behind him with a tray of glasses. "I think this is in order."

Nash took the bottle and glanced at the label. "Nice brand."

Gideon shrugged. "Penny picked it out."

Penny came up beside her husband. "You all deserve the best. And trust me, no one would have wanted to drink what he picked out."

Gideon brushed a kiss on her upturned mouth. "I already thanked you."

Trenton made a gagging sound. His wife, Ginny, admonished him, but Trenton ignored it. "No one wants to hear that."

Nash popped the cork. "That's my line. Penny's my sister, after all."

Trenton absently took his wife's hand in his. Ginny took a seat beside him. "But Penny is like a sister to me."

Gideon took the tray from Lilah. "It's the only reason you're still alive, pretty boy."

Isaac pulled Lilah to him. "As the newest married couple here, we're the ones who are supposed to be making everyone uncomfortable with public displays of affection."

Penny shook her head. "Gideon and I have been married for less than two years, you know."

Lilah rested her head on Isaac's shoulder. "Yep. An old married couple for sure."

Trenton helped Nash hand out the filled glasses. "I won't even ask what Ginny and I are."

Nash passed out the rest. "Parents."

Trenton smiled. "That we are. Only ones, too."

Gideon hushed the group. "All right, Prince Nash. A toast is in order, and you get the honors as Cantwell's fearless leader."

Trenton lifted his glass. "Without him, Isaac would still be making a fortune."

Isaac snickered. "That I would. I outdid myself."

Lilah kissed him. "That you did."

Trenton opened his mouth, and Nash stopped him.

"Don't even say what I know you're thinking."

Trenton used his innocent face. "All I was going to say was it isn't that hard to do."

Gideon hushed them again.

Nash looked at his family. "It's been a long road for all of us. And I don't mean Cantwell. But Cantwell wouldn't exist if it weren't for every one of you. You each brought life to the game: life to the characters, and life and depth to the story. Isaac, your book is amazing. You amaze me. Trenton, your photographs and vision of what Isaac wrote are unequaled. Gideon, you brought the women to life. Your art completed the vision of what Cantwell could be. And Lilah, your art brought the men to life. The expertise you brought not only made the game better but kept me on track and showed me how much bigger Cantwell could be. Congratulations to all of us."

Everyone took a sip of the champagne. Nash felt emotions clog his chest.

Trenton stood. "And to Prince Nash. Whose pretty face will keep selling the game for years to come."

The group cheered. "To Prince Nash!"

Nash swallowed the rest of his champagne. Before he could speak, Gideon's phone rang.

Gideon quickly left the room.

Penny stood but didn't follow. "He's supposed to have the week off."

Trenton came and put an arm around her. "I'm sure it's nothing."

Isaac offered Penny his support. "Gideon is and will always be the protector."

Nash didn't speak, but dread filled his stomach. There was only one thing that would pull Gideon away today.

Isaac stood between Nash and the doorway Gideon exited. "What aren't you telling us?"

Trenton came and stood behind Isaac. "Spill it, Camhion."

Penny took Nash's hand. "We don't have to do this today."

Nash looked at the ceiling. "Highs and lows. Isn't that what life is?"

Penny put her palm on his cheek. "And today is a high. It doesn't have to be a low."

Gideon came in. Everyone turned to look at him.

Nash tucked his hands in his black trouser pockets. "Well?"

Gideon kept his eyes on Nash. "I have to go. We can talk about it later. Keep watching the money roll in."

Nash's eyes darkened, and his voice shook with anger. "It's not about money, and you know it."

Isaac, the voice of reason, chimed in. "It's about bringing something fun and entertaining into the world. Something that makes you think outside yourself, think bigger than the world around you. And when needed, take you out of yourself. Let's focus on that. Gideon, you go do what you need to do."

Gideon hesitated. But when Penny nodded, he nodded back. "Congrats to all of us. I'll be back."

Penny hugged Nash as Gideon left. "So, are you finally going to let me play it?"

Nash kissed his sister's cheek. "You have to buy a copy."

Penny stood on her tiptoes. "I already did. Let's play."

* * *

Freya met Gideon in the hallway. Her face was pale, and she needed a shower, but there was nothing she could, or was, going to do about that right now. She kept her arms around her waist, her body shivering.

Gideon looked her over from head to toe. "Captain didn't share a lot of details. You look like you were in a scuffle."

Freya glanced at her knees. The pants were torn, and her knees were scraped. A nurse was kind enough to clean and bandage them when she refused to be admitted.

She blew a lock of hair out of her face. "I was out with Donna. We were having a drink. Well, I was having a drink. Donna stuck to sparkling water. We were discussing the case. She went outside to refill the meter. She'd left her phone in the car. She was gone too long, so I went to look for her."

Gideon took her arm and led her to the waiting area. He pushed her into a chair. "Where was she?"

"Alley. Just around the corner from where we'd parked. It was early afternoon, but I'd just come off the night shift, so we stopped for food. It looks like someone hit her on the back of the head. I took a few samples while waiting for the paramedics. Wood, I think."

Gideon took out a notepad. "So how did you tear your pants and bruise your face?"

Freya touched a finger to her cheek. It ached, but she

wasn't worried. "I came out of the alley to keep an eye out. I didn't want to move Donna, in case she had a neck injury. All I could do was drape my jacket over her and wait. When I got outside, there was a man in the shadows across the way. I had my badge, so I waved him over. I couldn't see his face, but he raised his hand and flipped me off. I figured he was just a punk kid. I don't carry a gun, but he didn't know that. I rested my hand under my jacket and started heading his way. When I got closer, he was wearing a black face mask over the lower portion of his face. And he wasn't a kid."

Gideon swore. "Tell me you didn't follow him."

Freya dropped her hand. "No. I couldn't leave Donna. But when I stepped back, he pulled a knife out of his pocket. Wicked looking thing. Not a pocketknife. Like a hunting knife. Non-serrated, curved, with a slight hook on one side. Looked old."

Gideon swore again. "You got a good look at the knife?"

"Yeah. It was like he was showing it off. I froze. I'm not a cop, Detective. I saw the knife, and I couldn't move."

Gideon crouched down in front of her. "Anyone would. You were smart to try to back off."

She took a shaky breath. "He rushed me. I thought for sure I was a goner. He slammed me in the shoulder hard enough to knock me down. Knocked the breath out of me. My cheek hit something, but I don't know what. I was dazed, but not bad. I crawled over to Donna. She had her gun. I know how to use one. But the man didn't come back."

Gideon excused himself for a moment. Freya got herself

back under control. She'd been scared, but she was okay. Donna was not. Gideon came back and took a seat in the chair next to her. He had a clipboard and printer paper. She saw the way he was holding the pencil. "Going to sketch the knife?"

"Going to try."

Freya watched his hands as he sketched an outline. "Longer. The edge with the hook was straight. The other side was more curved. The handle looked like worn wood. Maybe bone. The knife was probably steel but was patterned. Not smooth and shiny. The tip of the knife almost looked like an arrowhead; the hook was about a third deep."

Gideon shaded it in as she described the metal. "Steel would be likely. Wonder if it was handmade. Handle could also be antler. Not uncommon in a hunting knife."

Freya looked over his arm. "That's right. I'm not a knife expert. But this was not a household knife. Not military either."

Gideon snapped a photo of the drawing. "We'll pull some books for you to look at. See if we can narrow it down."

Freya knew cops. "You also want to see if a matching knife could have cut those boys."

Gideon folded the drawing. "Yeah. The knife used was likely a hunting knife. Blade approximately six to eight inches. According to the files, the cuts were clean. Other than dirt and debris from where the boys were held, nothing else was in the wounds. No other DNA was introduced via the knife. And like you said, the knife was smooth, not serrated. It was not your average kitchen knife."

Freya's mouth went dry. "So why didn't he kill me?"

Gideon looked down the hall where Donna was. "What is Agent Monaco's prognosis?"

"Good. The doctor is optimistic. He is keeping her unconscious because there is swelling in her brain. He doesn't think she'll need surgery, but time will tell. He thinks she'll wake up when he stops the meds, but right now he wants her quiet and still. Her parents are on their way."

"We can only hope she got a better look at him. I'll need your impression of height, weight, hair color, brow color, and what he was wearing."

Freya closed her eyes. "Denim. Dark. Windbreaker in navy, I think. Not black. He wore a baseball cap. Washington Capitals. A dime a dozen. Brown hair, not overly dark. Hat covered most of it. Dark brows, probably the same color as his hair. Older man, probably fifties. I could see wrinkles around his eyes. Maybe one-sixty. Under six feet. Average. Nothing special about him."

Gideon pulled out another sheet of paper and started sketching what she saw.

Freya wished she had seen more. "Not very helpful. And face masks are so common these days; no one would question why he was wearing one. It was black, too, if that helps."

Gideon smiled a little. "Not particularly. But the rest does. All parts of the puzzle. Have you spoken to your friend's superior?"

"No. I called dispatch. Barnes called me and asked what

happened. He said he was sending you over. Barnes likely spoke with the FBI, but he didn't say."

"We'll need to know if she's working on any other cases. Who else is she working with?"

Freya took the clipboard and wrote down what she knew. "She is working with an Agent Lorenzo. He's assigned to a desk; he's in a wheelchair after a bad shooting. But he's a whiz with the computer. He's been doing a lot of the legwork from his desk. As far as active cases, she tied one up a couple of weeks ago. This case has taken priority. But she would have enemies, same as you. Maybe this guy didn't care about me. Was just taunting me."

Gideon contemplated the picture. "Taunting, yes. I don't like the feel of it. This feels…"

Freya interrupted. "Same. This feels like our guy."

He glanced at her. "Yeah. It feels like our guy."

Gideon stayed with her until Donna's parents arrived. Freya gave them an abbreviated rundown of what happened. Donna's dad was a retired cop. She had no doubt he would get the full story out of Donna's unit chief.

Gideon came over. "Need a ride?"

Freya grabbed her bag. "Yes, I could use a ride. My car is at the station."

Gideon gestured for her to follow.

Exhaustion taking over, she yawned as she buckled in. "How did the launch go? I was watching it on the web. It's being called a contender for Game of the Year."

Gideon smiled. "Nash had a vision. He played a lot of games when we were younger. He'd lose himself inside role-playing game after role-playing game. Always wanted to be a hero. He talked about making his own game when we were kids. He worked for his dad for a while. He worked a few odd jobs, too. Has a law degree but never took the exams. Then of course, there was his misspent youth."

Freya rested her head. "I remember his modeling days."

Gideon snorted at that. "Pretty boy. He was smart enough to survive it. And he was smart enough to go back to college and at least get a bachelor's degree. That's where he learned a lot about game development. Filled in the gaps himself. Isaac's book gave him the perfect story, and he ran with it."

"I wanted to call him, but so much has happened."

Gideon glanced at her. "He'd like to see you."

Freya felt her cheeks heat. Remembering what had happened the first time she went to his house still kept her awake at night.

Gideon just shook his head. "Yep. Let's go say hello."

Freya wanted to tell him to take her back to the station. That she wasn't ready. But when would she be? "That would be nice."

Twenty minutes later, they were pulling into the driveway of a stately home across from Nash's. She climbed out of the car. "This one yours?"

Gideon glanced at the house. "Penny's. So I guess it's mine now, too. I had an apartment before I moved in."

"I had a nice condo in Virginia. Pained me to let it go when I moved to D.C. I can't imagine living in a house that big."

Gideon shrugged. "You get used to it. But Nash

converted the upstairs for Cantwell's offices when he bought his. Not much use for a family home if you don't want a family. But he loves the house. After living in the Camhion family home growing up, this is modest in comparison."

Freya only heard the part about not wanting a family. "I didn't pay much attention to the house the one time I was here. Donna was on her way out, and I knew Nash wasn't going to be happy about it."

"No, he wasn't. Deep down he had hoped his attacker was long dead. Finding out the man was still alive was difficult. Nash wears his feelings. You'll know how he's feeling at any given moment."

"Yeah, I got that. I guess we'll see what he's feeling today."

Gideon gave her an odd glance but didn't say anything. He opened the front door. "Just where I left you."

Penny came and hugged him. "My parents sent dinner in congratulations. Nash is putting it together."

Freya stepped inside. Several eyes came her way. The only one she had met before was Lilah.

"Freya. It's so nice that you could come." Lilah jumped up and came over to hug her.

A little surprised by the hug, she didn't hug her back. Lilah let her go before she could respond. "Hope I'm not intruding. I've heard so much about the launch; I wanted to congratulate Nash in person."

Gideon closed the door. "Only with a tiny nudge."

Freya greeted everyone and shook hands. "It's nice to meet all of you."

Ginny came over and hugged her as well. "We owe you a lot. You're welcome to join us for dinner. Eldridge sent over enough food to feed an army."

Penny shook her hand, giving her a once over. "Dad never does things in half measures. You'll find my brother much the same. It is nice to finally meet you. I never got to thank you in person for what you did for me, either."

Uncomfortable with the praise, Freya shrugged. "I just share what the evidence says."

Nash was wiping his hands on a towel when he came in. "Dinner is ready. Mom sent dessert. Penny, your favorite. Though seems unfair. It's my party…"

Freya stopped in her tracks when Nash's eyes found hers and his words cut off. His eyes showed her exactly what he was feeling. Hunger. Stunned by the look, she had to clear her throat before she spoke. "Hi. Hope you don't mind me coming. Congratulations on the game. I was watching it on the web."

His eyes went dark. Then they went to Gideon. "What happened?"

Gideon shook his head, his tone firm. "After dinner."

Freya kept her eyes on Nash as he came her way. She had to tip her head up when he got close enough to touch her cheek. "It's fine."

His fingers drifted down her cheek. His hand trembled.

She wasn't sure how long they stared at each other.

Penny broke the trance. "Come on, we're starving. You can catch up after we eat."

Nash took her hand and led her to the kitchen. The large table next to a bay window was loaded with food. Nash pulled out a chair. "Italian."

Freya looked up at him. "Your favorite?"

"Yeah. You'll like it. Same place I sent to you."

The other three couples took a seat. Freya realized everyone was staring at them. "I should wash up first."

Nash pointed to the hall. "First door on the left."

Freya quickly sought the sanctuary of the bathroom. She took a look in the mirror. Her hair was mussed, the bruise on her cheek was starting to form, and her face had a couple of smudges. Her blouse was untucked from when she'd removed her jacket, and her pants were torn and bloody. Not exactly the first impression she wanted to make. She combed out her hair, washed off the dirt, and did her best to straighten her clothes. Her knees were aching, and her head was hurting.

A knock interrupted her. Gideon's voice echoed through the door. "Top shelf."

Freya opened the cabinet. She gratefully grabbed the bottle and shook out a couple of tablets. "Got them. Thanks."

"Come on out. You look fine."

Freya opened the door. "An expert on women, huh?"

Gideon shrugged. "I have a mom, a sister, and a wife. Let's just say I know enough."

She came back to the table, swallowed the tablets, and dug into the plate someone had fixed for her. Conversation was lively, most centering around the game and Isaac's book. Several of them shared their favorite quotes of the day. Trenton ragged on Isaac. Gideon smiled more than she'd ever seen him, and the women were genuinely happy and proud of their husbands.

Freya didn't have much to add to the conversation. She stopped mid-bite when Isaac spoke to her.

"How long have you lived in D.C., Freya? Delilah told me you used to work for a large lab in Virginia."

She glanced at the group who were all now looking at her. "Not quite three years. My grandma passed, so I moved here. My grandparents raised me, so I wanted to be here for Grandpa Henry."

Lilah placed a hand on hers. "Sorry to hear that. I didn't know."

Freya swallowed the lump in her throat at the memory of her grandma. "Anyway, I got bored pretty fast, so I took the job offered at the police department. A lab's a lab."

Trenton jumped in. "Bet the pay was better at the private lab. If you're ever looking to invest, I'm your guy."

Ginny's head shook. "Ignore him. He's always looking for new clients. Though he is your guy if you do."

Freya glanced around. "Where's your daughter?"

Ginny pointed upstairs. "She and my brother have been playing Cantwell since school let out. I figured we would eat and then bring some food up. My brother isn't comfortable in crowds."

They finished up dinner. Nash pushed everyone out of the kitchen before heading back in. Freya found herself sitting beside Isaac. "I wanted to tell you I'm a fan of your work. I can't wait to read Cantwell. I read a little during lunch."

"Thank you. Are you going to tell us why your face is bruised, your pants are torn, and you came in with Gideon?"

Freya opened her mouth, but Gideon spoke.

"Open case. Can't talk about it."

Freya nodded. "Right. Open case. Can't talk about it."

Isaac's mouth tightened. "Sure. But we can."

Freya stood. "I'm going to go help."

She heard voices rising as Gideon refused to talk about how they had come to show up together. She found Nash loading the dishwasher. "Let me help."

Nash came around the island counter. His hands wove into her hair. "I'm glad you came."

Freya looked into his eyes. "Me, too."

Nash bent his head, and Freya rose up on her toes to meet him halfway. She sighed into his mouth as his lips closed over hers. She wound her arms around his neck and pressed her breasts against his chest. She opened her mouth to his when his tongue traced the seam of her lips.

Nash spun so that she was backed up against the island. His knee found its way between her thighs. Mindlessly, she pressed herself against him. His hands tugged her shirt from her waistband and found the skin of her back. His fingers tightened on her waist as she twisted closer.

Angry words from the living room split them apart. She would have fallen if the island hadn't been behind her.

Nash ran a hand through his long black hair. "We should go. Isaac has lost patience. Penny is probably starting to freak out a little."

She tucked her blouse back in as Nash finger-combed her hair back into place. "They're going to know what we were doing in here."

Nash brushed his lips against hers one last time. "Yeah.

They are. Come on."

Freya had no choice but to follow when he grabbed her hand and tugged her along.

Isaac's arms were crossed over his chest. "Fine. So you were investigating Cormac's murder. That's not new. You've been investigating it for years."

Nash kept Freya at his side. "All right. Enough. What I tell you doesn't leave this room. I don't want a word of it to make its way to my parents. Understood?"

The whole room nodded in unison. Freya squeezed Nash's hand.

Nash took a deep breath. "Freya went digging in the department's evidence room. She wanted to look over the original evidence in my grandfather's case. She found a box of evidence."

Isaac nodded. "Glad nothing is lost; it happens in cases this old."

Nash reluctantly shook his head. "My evidence. Not Grandfather's."

That got the room talking, except for Penny, who watched her brother closely. Nash looked like he didn't know what to say next. Freya nudged him. He nodded at her.

Freya spoke. "The evidence contained Nash's attacker's DNA. I processed it, and it came back with a match to an unknown suspect in twelve other cases, one recent one right here in D.C. I called a friend of mine at the FBI, Donna Monaco. She's been looking into Cormac Camhion's murder and Nash's ties to the other boys who were attacked. Twelve other boys, teenagers Nash's age when he was attacked, were kidnapped, tortured, and murdered."

Penny gasped. Every ounce of color drained from her face. "What?"

Gideon hugged her to him. "One of them was less than a year ago. Freya is now assigned to work on the case in conjunction with the FBI to process evidence and to try to do a forensic genealogy search, much like she did to find Trenton's cult members."

Freya stuck to the facts and tried to ignore the emotions in the room. "Tonight Donna was attacked outside of the restaurant where we were having lunch. The attacker hit her in the back of the head, knocking her unconscious. I went to find her, and a man who I believe was her attacker was nearby. He fled the scene, and in the process, knocked me down."

Trenton took Ginny's hand. "The face and the knees."

Freya nodded but wasn't sure she should give any more details. Thankfully Gideon took over.

"I met Freya at the hospital. Agent Monaco is in the ICU, but the doctors think she'll recover. Freya didn't get a good look at the attacker because he wore a face mask. The medical kind. We both think this is our guy. Donna is investigating thirteen homicides and Nash's kidnapping. He pulled out a knife. A very distinct one. He made no move to use it on Freya or Donna. Not his M.O."

Nash gagged. "No. They're not teenage boys."

Gideon kept his distance as Nash pulled it together. "She got a good look at it. I made sketches of it and the man. The FBI will investigate the attack on their agent. I don't believe in coincidences. I think the man knew exactly who he attacked: the agent investigating his case."

Ginny, the reporter that she was, spoke up. "Do you think he knows Freya is the forensic expert investigating it?"

Gideon nodded. "I'd say there's a good chance. Something in the way he approached the women and taunted Freya by showing her the knife says he does."

Freya described it. "It was a unique piece. I'll look over the books on knives when I'm back in the lab. I know I can get a close match."

Nash turned her to face him. "No."

Gideon took a step closer but stopped. "Nash. This is how it works. He got cocky. He showed himself. He might make a mistake. One we can use to our advantage."

Freya took one of his hands in hers. "Let me do my job. Let me help find him."

Nash pulled away and left the room.

Penny started to go after him, but Gideon pulled her back. "Let him be. He has to work this out his way. He wants this over. He wants justice for Cormac and those other boys. But another part of him wants to deny it ever happened. I swear this time we'll find him."

Freya glanced back at the doorway Nash exited. "I should go."

Gideon's dark gaze found hers. "I'll drive you back to the station. Penny, please go home. Everyone else, do the same. Leave him be."

Chapter Six

The next morning, Gideon found Nash at the gym. Nash saw Gideon come in and waved him over. Gideon grabbed a pair of sparring gloves and joined him. "Thought I'd find you here when you weren't at home."

Nash tightened his gloves. "Sometimes it really cramps a man's style to have his best friend and sister spying on him."

"Nah. You have no style."

Nash swung first. Gideon expertly blocked him. "You might be right. I certainly haven't been charming the ladies lately."

Gideon feinted and jabbed, hitting Nash's arm when he blocked. He grunted when Nash landed a blow. "It's harder when the lady matters."

Distracted, Gideon's left hook caught Nash in the stomach. "Eginhard's words of wisdom?"

Gideon spun, blocked Nash's leg sweep, then hit Nash in the midsection, taking him to the mat. "I would know. It took me years to admit I needed Penny. Even then, I was hesitant to do anything about it."

Nash bucked until he was free. He got to his feet and crouched. "You were in love with her for twenty years. Honestly, it was painful to watch."

Gideon matched Nash move for move. "She wasn't ready. Neither was I."

Nash deflected Gideon's spin kick and went in low. "So what? You think I just need time?"

Gideon grunted when Nash successfully got past his guard. This time, Gideon hit the mat. "I was afraid. I was afraid I wasn't good enough. That deep down, I wasn't what she needed. You have the same fears, Nash."

Nash had heard much the same from his father. That he feared too much. That he let the past have too much control. With a low roar, he flipped Gideon over and got him in a lock hold.

Despite Gideon's size, Nash's grip on him didn't break. After a few minutes, Gideon reluctantly tapped out.

Nash let him go and got to his feet. His breathing was heavy. "Fear. I've known too many forms of it, Gideon. I was afraid of the man who attacked me. I was afraid of strangers. I was afraid to go anywhere but school and home. When I got older, I was afraid I'd lose my parents. Afraid I'd lose my friends. Afraid that a woman would get too close. And one did. And I lost her. I feared for my sister when my cousin tried to kill her. I feared for Trenton when that woman and her son tried to kill him. I feared for Lilah and Isaac when Avery tried to kill them."

Gideon tugged off the gloves. "You loved Maggie. I wish I had gotten a chance to meet her. Trenton was the only one."

Nash stripped off his gloves and tossed them. Gideon followed him as he headed for the locker room. "Maggie seems so long ago. She made everything seem better. I met her a month after I left home. I couldn't take my parents hovering anymore. I needed to get away. When that modeling agency signed me, it was simply a way to survive. I had no other skills or talents. Just a pretty face. And nice abs, or so my agent said. So in a way, it was your fault. All that working out you made us do."

Gideon smiled in remembrance. "Trenton followed you. Well, sometimes. He had wandering feet, too. I was already looking forward to the academy. And Isaac, well, we now know where he ended up for a couple of years."

"Still hard to believe he worked for the Pentagon. Seems like a bad joke."

Gideon stopped him. "You only had Maggie for two years. We were all there for you when she died. No matter what you do, no matter where you go, we're still here."

Nash scrubbed his face with his hands. "I know. Things had started settling down when Freya found that damn evidence box."

"So why not Freya? First, she's not like the other women you've dated. Thank goodness. I don't think I could handle another Candy, or Muffy, or whatever the heck fluffy names these women call themselves."

"You forgot Jilly and Tilly."

Gideon's eyes closed for a second. "Those two. I wasn't sure I should be proud of you for daring to date those twins, or shudder in revulsion at how dumb they were."

Nash took off his sweaty t-shirt and took a seat, silent laughter shaking his shoulders. "Stick with proud. Seems mean to call them dumb. They weren't that bad."

Gideon tossed Nash a towel. "Yeah, they were."

Nash conceded. "Okay, they were. But they were pretty cute; you have to admit."

Gideon dipped his head. "Look, unless you have something against happiness, I think you and Freya make sense. She's not a social climber. She's cute. Cuter than Jilly and Tilly combined. She's smart. And she likes you for you. Not because of the Camhion last name. Or your bank account. What else do you need?"

It was a good question. One Nash couldn't answer. Gideon had a way of seeing past his words to what was truly inside. "Then what? We get married and live happily ever after?"

Gideon held up his ring finger. "And why not? You pushed me to take a hard look at my life. To take a risk before it was too late. And the end result was Penny. I got the better end of the deal."

Nash thought of his sister. "Yeah, you did. But I told her she couldn't do better than you. If I were a woman, I'd marry you."

Gideon snorted at that. "You're not my type. Too pretty."

Nash gave Gideon a quick hug. "Go. I'm fine. I'm still trying to get past the fact that the man who attacked me might have had his hands on Freya. But I'm dealing with it. Part of me really hopes it was just some wacko after her friend."

Gideon's eyes darkened. "And yet we both know better."

Nash nodded. "No coincidences."

"No."

* * *

Nash spent the rest of the day working. The tech team was fielding a few post-launch bugs, but nothing major. He had started a new game, and he was still amazed at the breadth of the story, the beauty of the colors, and the world that the quartet had created.

When his phone rang, he smiled. "Dad. Are you and Mom home?"

Eldridge Camhion's voice was loud over the phone. "Got in about an hour ago. Your mother is outside fussing with her flowers. I've been following the news. Your company is doing quite well."

"We're all happy. Nary a negative review. At least, none I'll read."

Eldridge approved. "Good. Even bad press can be good press. But from what I've seen, there's not a lot of negative. I read Isaac's book. He gets more brilliant by the day."

"That he does. So what's up?"

Eldridge paused. "Hayden's back in the hospital. I got word from Penny when I called in to check on her."

Nash's knee-jerk reaction was disgust. Hayden Brooks was everything he disliked wrapped into one package. He was only an uncle through marriage. His daughter, Clara, who was not a blood relative either, had attempted to kidnap and kill Penny. In the end, Gideon stopped Clara. A bullet had a way of doing that. After Clara died, Hayden seemed genuinely distraught. But he had betrayed the Camhion family. He stole money, tried to smear the Camhion name, and Eldridge had bailed him out. Years later, his father accepted Hayden's apology, but Nash didn't trust him. And he didn't believe him.

Nash bit back the words he wanted to say. "I take it he's on death's door again."

Eldridge ignored the sarcastic tone. "He was released, so not today. I know you're not pleased with him working for Camhion Enterprises again."

Nash tried to loosen the tension in his shoulders. "It's Penny's company now. If she is okay with it, then who am I to argue. Just keep him on a tight leash. It worries me having him back in the family fold."

Eldridge changed the subject. "Anyway, we got your invitation to Gideon's birthday party next week. Penny is on cloud nine helping to plan it."

Nash and Penny had tag-teamed him. In the end, he agreed. But Nash knew it was only because Penny had convinced him. Gideon had been dodging birthday parties since he turned eighteen, and he only went to those earlier parties because his mother and sister threw them. "We're all looking forward to it. I take it this phone call is to RSVP."

The sound of his dad's low hum came over the line. "Actually, I'm curious about a woman named Freya."

Figured. Nash should have known Penny would mention her to their parents. "She's a friend."

"You always were a difficult child. Penny seems to think she's more than a friend. And Penny seems to approve. She said she was the woman who found that crazy cultist who was after Trenton."

Nash gave in. "Yes, she is. And she helped find the woman after Isaac and Lilah. Yes, I like her. No, I am not dating her. No, I haven't met her parents. Or, in her case, her grandpa."

"Sounds serious."

Nash shook his head. "That is what you would hear."

Eldridge pushed. "Nash, you're my son. I want nothing more than for you to be happy. Your mother and I have been happily married for forty-five years. I wouldn't trade a single moment. Gideon might not be who I would have picked for Penny, but he makes her happy. He would protect her, and has, with his life. As a father, there is nothing more precious than my children."

Nash had heard this speech before. But for some reason, today it hit home. "I know my kidnapping has weighed on you all these years. But you can't predict the future any more than I can. You would never have given up looking for me. I love you, Dad."

Eldridge's voice cracked. "I love you. Enough of that. I'm looking forward to meeting her at Gideon's birthday party. Your mom sends her love, and we'll see you there."

"Bye." Nash tapped his phone for a moment. He then sent out a quick text, along with a time and an address.

A couple of hours later, he had his answer.

* * *

Nash had outdone himself, if he did say so himself. Gideon's fortieth birthday party was well underway. People were laughing, drinks were flowing, and the vegetarian menu was plentiful. Gideon and his sister were slow dancing and acting like newlyweds. They were surrounded by dozens of other couples, but Gideon stood head and shoulders above everyone around him and couldn't be missed. Isaac and Lilah were chatting and laughing with Trenton and Ginny.

Nash grabbed a glass of champagne and took his first sip of the night. His work was now done, and it was time to enjoy himself. His smoky gaze did a turn around the room. There were plenty of people here he didn't know. Friends and colleagues Gideon worked with mingled with their friends and family. He saw his parents and waved but didn't make his way over to them. He'd chatted with them earlier. He saw Gideon's mom, Miranda, and his sister, Iris. Iris lifted her champagne glass to him in a small toast. He smiled and returned it but kept walking the perimeter of the room. Even Isaac's mom was in attendance. Since her husband had been arrested, she'd been trying to build a relationship with her son. Nash wasn't sure how he felt about it, but Isaac was willing, so Nash kept his opinion to himself.

He grabbed a plate and mingled among the guests as he kept his eyes out for the woman he was looking for. Another hour passed, but Freya hadn't made an appearance. He grabbed another glass of champagne, and this one he downed in two gulps.

"Problem?" Iris Eginhard looped her arm through his.

Nash set the empty glass down and led Iris to the dance floor. She was a tiny thing at five feet even compared to his six feet. She was a smaller, more feminine version of her brother. Her long black hair was plaited down her back, her brown eyes framed by dark lashes, and her figure curvy. But as they danced, he held her at a distance. His feelings for her had always been brotherly.

Iris looked up at him. "Women troubles?"

Nash spun and dipped her. "I don't have women troubles."

Iris gripped his shoulder. "Then why the frown?"

Nash ignored the question. "So how does it feel to have a brother who's forty?"

Iris glanced over at her brother and Penny. "I don't know. I'll have to ask Penny how she feels when you turn forty."

Nash made a face. He was just three months behind. He released Iris when the dance ended, and they made their way over to Gideon. Nash hugged his sister and clapped Gideon on the back. "You still have some moves for an old man."

Penny, a little tipsy, wrapped her arm around her husband's waist. She gazed up at him adoringly. "He sure does. And I can't wait until we get home and he shows me."

Nash saw Gideon's eyes heat. "This is where I leave."

Iris kissed Gideon's cheek. "Same. I'm going to go flirt with one of your friends."

Gideon's gaze jumped from his wife to his sister. "Which one?"

Iris gave a wave to one of the officers standing by the buffet table. "Your friend, Montgomery."

Gideon glared at the man across the room. "He's a good cop. Lots of potential."

Iris kissed his cheek again, then hugged Penny and Nash. "Have a good night. And stop glaring at him. He's been a perfect gentleman."

Gideon growled. "And he had better keep it that way."

Nash agreed. "Let me know if he gets out of line."

Iris let out an exasperated sigh and made her way across the room.

Penny grabbed her husband's arm and leaned against him. "He's going to make a great father one day. Soon, I hope. We could get started on it when we get home."

Gideon leaned down and whispered something in her ear that made her blush. He then turned dark eyes to Nash. "I haven't thanked you yet for the party. Not sure how we'll top this when you turn forty."

Nash made an appropriate comment and excused himself. He could feel Gideon's eyes on him, but he didn't turn back. No doubt Gideon would make a great father. The man was steady as a rock. And his sister would make a wonderful mother. She would bring the next generation of Camhions into the world. It was a sobering thought. There was so much evil in the world. But Gideon would keep his children safe. He would teach them to be able to defend themselves, just like he had the quartet and his sister. No doubt Penny had gotten a few lessons, too.

Needing some fresh air, Nash stepped outside. He strolled along the pathways around the hotel where the party was being held. He was making his way back to the front when he heard his name.

"Nash?"

That voice. That soft, smoky, silky voice. He turned to see Freya standing a few feet from him. Tonight her layered blonde hair was loose around her shoulders, with bangs framing her oval face. Her hazel eyes were enhanced with eyeshadow and mascara, her full lips tinted a pale pink. Her knee-length white dress, tied with a silver sash, blew in the breeze. A small gold locket hung above the V-neck of the strapless bodice. Her toned legs were exposed by the dress, and on her feet were a pair of dainty silver heels. She was quite simply lovely.

Nash was hardly aware that he had stepped closer to her. She smiled at him, her eyes a little unsure. Then she stumbled a bit as her sandal slid on the gravel. He quickly grasped her arm to steady her. He caught her faint floral scent in the breeze.

Freya righted herself. "Sorry. I'm not used to heels. Not exactly appropriate at work."

Nash brushed a tendril of hair away from her cheek. Now that she was in front of him again, he was at a loss for words.

Freya kept her eyes on his. "Are you okay?"

Nash mentally shook his head. "Sorry. It was getting stuffy in there, so I came outside to get some air. I was worried you changed your mind."

Freya turned when three men came outside. Nash saw her body tense, then relax. He turned to see Gideon, Trenton, and Isaac coming toward them.

Gideon smiled, the concern that was in his eyes fading. "Now I see why you snuck out. Hi, Freya. Glad you could make it."

Freya waved at the trio and smiled at Gideon. "Happy birthday. Sorry I'm late. I got stuck in the lab. And it took me forever to get home to change."

Gideon's eyes sharpened. "Bad?"

Freya gave a tired shrug. "Bad enough. But you're off

duty, Detective."

Trenton came forward. "It's nice to see you again."

Isaac seconded that. "Glad you could make it. Delilah was looking forward to chatting again."

When Nash just stared, Gideon kicked his shoe. "Nash, why don't you take Freya inside and see that she eats. If I know her, she hasn't eaten all day."

Nash held his elbow out. "Shall we?"

Freya took his arm and used him for balance as they made their way inside. She glanced around as they headed toward the food, and she waved at people she knew. "I didn't know Detective Eginhard knew so many people."

Nash handed her a plate. "He does tend to be a loner. But despite himself, he has a lot of friends. My parents are here, since they're also his in-laws. His mom and sister are here, too. His sister Iris is off somewhere with an Officer Montgomery."

Freya eyed the buffet and made a few selections. "Good choice."

Nash stepped into her line of sight. "Really?"

She looked up at him through her lashes. "If I were ten years younger, maybe."

Lust punched him in the gut. "More like five."

She shrugged a bare shoulder. "I go for older men. I hear you'll be forty next."

"Three months. I know it's rude to ask a lady her age."

Freya made a few more selections and filled her plate. "Thirty-five, since you didn't ask."

Nash carried her plate to where his friends were sitting.

Freya took a seat when Nash held her chair. "Hi,

everyone. Sorry I'm so late."

Penny sat staring at Freya. "It's uncanny."

Ginny looked at Penny, then at Freya. Her scrutiny intensified. "You're right."

Freya frowned. "Do I have something on my face?"

Penny spoke. "No, nothing on your face. You look like someone."

Gideon glanced at his wife. "Penny."

She tipped her face up to kiss him. "I hadn't put it together last time we met her. But you're right. And you were right on three out of four. It was only a matter of time."

Freya set her fork down. "Am I missing something?"

Nash glared at his friends. "Enough."

Penny giggled. She laid her head on her husband's shoulder and gave Freya a huge smile. "Sorry. I think I might be drunk. And I'm hoping Gideon takes advantage as soon as we're in the car."

Trenton handed her a glass of water. "You only think you're drunk?"

Nash glanced at Ginny and Lilah, who were both now staring at Freya. "Just forget it, you two."

Penny just gave him a look of contentment. "Never say never, brother. Gideon, it's getting late, isn't it?"

Nash waved them off. "No one will even notice you left."

Lilah whispered in her husband's ear.

Isaac nodded. "Delilah and I both work in the morning. We should get going too."

Ginny popped up. "Same."

Trenton looked like he wanted to argue, but Ginny

grabbed him by the arm and tugged.

There was a final round of happy birthdays before the group disbanded.

Freya stopped mid bite. "Everyone's leaving?"

Nash glanced at his watch. "It's almost eleven."

Freya glanced around. The party was about half the size it had been a short while ago. An older couple was looking at them. She nudged Nash. "Your parents?"

Nash looked over. "Uh, yes. I give them thirty seconds before they come over. Sorry."

Freya glanced at him. "For what?"

"You'll see."

Nash's mother was the first to arrive. "Great party, Nash. Your father and I wanted to come say hello to your friend."

Freya wiped her hands on her napkin and rose. "Freya Jensen. I work with Gideon."

Nash's father gave her a skeptical once over. "I'm Eldridge Camhion, and this is my wife, Victoria. If I recall, you're not a police officer."

Freya was quick to respond as she shook their hands. "Forensic analyst. I work in the crime lab."

Victoria put two and two together. "Nash mentioned to his father that you're the one who helped Trenton and Isaac. My dear, we owe you a huge debt."

Freya's face looked stunned when Victoria grabbed her and hugged her. Nash sat back and watched. Eldridge settled for taking her hand. "We certainly do. We think of those boys as our own. Gideon, especially."

Eldridge and Victoria took a seat. Victoria waved at the

still full plate. "Please, don't let us interrupt."

Nash waved at a waiter and grabbed four glasses of champagne from the tray. "It's like eating in a fishbowl."

Freya took a sip of her champagne, glanced into the glass, and took another. "Wow. This is delicious."

Nash didn't take a drink of his. "Only the best, as my dad would say."

Victoria gave her son an odd look before turning back to Freya. "So, Freya, you work in the crime lab?"

Nash heard the tension in his mom's voice. "Mom."

Eldridge patted his wife's hand. "He's right. We're celebrating tonight."

Freya set her fork down. "I'm sorry. I feel like I'm missing something. Between Nash's friends and now you."

Nash closed his eyes for a moment. "This is my fault."

Victoria glanced between Nash and Freya. "Your fault about what, dear?"

Nash shrugged, not wanting to explain his relationship with Freya. The one he was starting to want more and more.

Freya glanced at Nash. "Well, it is getting late. I guess I should be going, too. Sorry to eat and run."

Nash glared at his parents and quickly followed Freya as she bolted for the door. "Freya, please. I'm sorry."

Freya slowed her pace as she dug her keys out of her purse. "Ever feel like everyone has a different script than you?"

Nash halted her, his eyes serious. "Yes. I do."

Freya took a deep breath. "Do you want to explain to me what's going on?"

Nash tucked his hands in his trouser pockets. "You look like a woman in a painting that I'm supposed to marry. And my parents hear the word forensic, and they have a visceral reaction. They can't help it."

Freya dropped her keys. She quickly stooped to pick them up. "You're not making any sense."

Nash took her hands in his. "You know Cantwell's storyline."

Freya nodded. "I finished Isaac's book. Started the game, too. It's a beautiful game."

Nash nodded, her simple praise warming him. "As you know, each hero has a heroine to rescue. The heroes look like the quartet. Gideon, Trenton, Isaac, and myself. Lilah drew them. Gideon drew four women, one for each hero. Penny, Ginny, and Lilah look like the heroines. You look like the fourth."

"Oh. That's nice, I guess." She started back to her car.

Nash halted her again. "Freya. Nothing between us has gone as planned. I jumped you the day we met. I was rude the next day. I asked you to help me when I didn't have the right to. And I'm sorry if my friends embarrassed you. And my parents. I was vague about who you were when I talked to my dad a few days ago. Penny mentioned you to them. I couldn't tell them the truth about the case. And I don't know where, if anywhere, our relationship is going. Texts and phone calls are not enough."

Freya's eyes softened. "Your friends didn't embarrass me. And no, texts and phone calls are not enough. Not anymore."

Nash ignored the knot in his stomach. He continued.

"It's hard on all of us. All these years not knowing who killed my grandfather. They know you work in the forensic lab, and they know Gideon looks into the case. I didn't want them to push you. My father hopes one day the police will find the man who murdered his dad."

Freya laid a hand on his shoulder. "You don't believe Gideon can catch him."

Nash's eyes darkened as the past tried to rear up. "I want to. But I do believe men can get away with murder. For myself, I can live without finding him. But for the other boys, for my dad, I want him found."

Freya moved closer so that her body was pressed to his, and she wrapped her arms around his waist. She didn't say anything; she just held him.

Nash felt the tension drain out of him. Freya's body was soft against his, her curves hugging the hard planes of his body. He shifted so that he could look down into her eyes. "I want to see you again. Dinner tomorrow?"

Freya's body trembled in his arms. "I just so happen to be free."

Nash released her and took a step back. "I don't know where you live."

Freya pulled out her phone. She texted him her address. "I'll see you tomorrow."

Nash walked Freya the rest of the way to her car. "Tomorrow."

Chapter Seven

Freya looked in the mirror and tried to give herself a pep talk. "Get a grip, Freya. It's just a date. You've had dates. It might have been a while, but it's like riding a bike. This is what you wanted when you started texting him. Besides that, he's already seen you naked."

Freya pulled the curlers out of her hair and watched as the curls immediately straightened. She felt her stomach sink but then simply brushed her hair out and put it in a twist. The first time she'd texted Nash Camhion, she had felt like a gawky teenager texting her crush. Once upon a time, Nash Camhion had been a teenage girl's dream. Not much had changed. Now he was a grown woman's dream.

Freya grabbed and tossed her underwear on the bed. The strapless bra and satin underwear were the nicest ones she had. Not that she planned on him seeing her underwear tonight. She then turned and stared into her closet. Maybe if she stared long enough, a suitable outfit would materialize.

Where would Nash take her to dinner? And what was she doing having dinner with Nash Camhion anyway? The guy was rich and gorgeous. His hair was the color of black smoke, his eyes an unusual gray. He was six feet of beautiful male. He rubbed shoulders with D.C.'s elite. She'd seen pictures of the women he dated. No doubt they had tons of appropriate clothes to go out with a man like Nash. Clothes were low on her priority list. She barely left her lab, didn't have many friends in D.C. besides Donna, and so she didn't have suitable clothes to go out with him. For pity's sake, she'd had to buy the white dress and the shoes she'd worn to Gideon's party because she didn't have a single dress in her closet.

The doorbell rang, and she closed her eyes. She glanced around for something to put on. She couldn't answer the door naked.

"I got it, sweetheart."

Freya poked her head out the bedroom door. "Grandpa, you should tell him I'm not here."

Henry Jensen made a clucking sound with his tongue. "I've been telling you for months now to get out there and make some friends. Now put some clothes on, and I'll let your friend in."

Freya closed the door and leaned against it. She figured she had two choices. She could chicken out and fake a cold, or she could put on the white dress she'd worn last night and go have dinner. Grateful she'd at least shaved her legs, she pulled on her underwear and the white dress. She stopped for a moment to admire the dress in the full-length mirror, then grabbed her grandma's shawl and wrapped it around her shoulders. Then she put on the locket she'd worn last night. A quick dab of lip gloss, a dusting of face powder, and a deep breath, she was ready.

Freya came into the living room where her grandpa was sitting and chatting with Nash. He had on a white dress shirt and a pair of dark slacks. The polish on his shoes practically shined. She gave him a small smile when he rose from his seat as she entered the room.

Nash handed her the pink roses he brought her. "Hi."

Freya felt her cheeks heating. "Hi."

Henry nudged her. "Shoes, Freya. You can't go out in bare feet."

She glanced down at her toes. "Right. Shoes."

She grabbed the sandals from last night. She slipped them on. "Let me go put these in a vase."

She tore off to the kitchen, a little wobbly on the heels, and glanced around for anything that would hold the flowers.

Henry pointed to the top cabinet. "Your grandma kept the vases in there. And I'll take care of it. Now go."

Freya handed him the flowers. "All right. I'm going."

Nash was waiting by the front door. "Ready?"

"Ready." She grabbed her purse and locked the door behind her.

Nash's arms came around her and pressed her up against the door. "Freya?"

She must have made some sort of yes sound because before she knew it, his fingers had tunneled through her hair, the careful twist of her hair fell, and his lips descended on hers. She wrapped her arms around his neck and kissed him back. His lips were firm on hers, and his breath tasted like toothpaste. She rose up on her toes to get a better taste.

A light flickering on and off on the porch made Nash pull away.

She dropped back onto her heels. "Jeez."

Nash cleared his throat. "Dinner."

Freya glanced back at the shadow of her grandpa in the window. "Right. Dinner."

Nash helped her into the car. The town car wasn't quite what she was expecting. She had expected a flashy sports car or some sort of exotic foreign car. She tried not to be impressed by the comfy seats, the electronic dash, or anything else. But she was.

Nash leaned over and touched her mouth. "Hungry?"

Freya swallowed the lump in her throat. She wasn't sure he was talking about food, but either way, the answer was the same. "Yes."

Freya didn't know what to say to him now that they were alone. When it was work, she knew what to say. She was confident. But this was a date, and all she could think about was the two of them naked. Thankfully the ride to the restaurant was a short one. Her heels clicked on the pavement as he guided her inside. Inevitably she stumbled a bit, but he simply kept her arm in his.

They were immediately seated at a private table. Freya glanced around. "This is very nice. I've never been here."

Nash handed her the menu. "How long did you say you've been in D.C.?"

Freya thanked him. Her eyes widened at the discreet prices. She stumbled over her words. "Almost three years."

Nash set a hand over hers. "We don't have to eat here. We don't have to do anything you don't want to do. Freya, if nothing else, I'd like to think we're friends."

Freya set the menu down. "We are friends. But I'm nervous. This is a date. Not a text, or a phone call, or work. That makes it different. You know, I didn't know who the

Camhion family was until I moved here. Nash, I'm just a lab tech. I don't eat in fancy restaurants; I don't own more than this one dress, and it's new. I don't wear heels, and I don't know what to say to you tonight."

Nash rose. He took her hand and pulled her to her feet. "Come on. Let's go."

Freya didn't have much choice since he didn't let go of her hand. When they got to the car, he stopped and dropped to her feet. She had to put her hands on his shoulders for balance when he took off her shoes. He then opened the car door, gently pushed her inside, and came around.

Nash glanced over at her. "Do you like Chinese food?"

Freya answered. "I do."

Nash drove a few blocks and left her in the car. Fifteen minutes later, he came back with a large sack of food. The smell of it made her mouth water. He handed her the bag.

Nash put the car in reverse.

She took a peek inside, but everything was in containers. "What are you doing?"

Nash shook his head. When he pulled into the driveway of her house, he got out and came around. "You hold the food. Don't forget your shoes."

Freya shrieked a bit when he picked her up and carried her to her front door. She fumbled with her keys and somehow managed to get the door open while holding the food and her sandals.

Nash set her down. "Good evening, Henry. Do you like Chinese food?"

Henry rose from his easy chair as Nash set Freya on her

feet. "I wasn't expecting you back so soon."

"Freya wasn't a fan of the restaurant I picked. Or her shoes. So we picked up dinner."

Henry saw the smile on his granddaughter's face. "So I see. Let's go eat."

The trio sat in the cozy kitchen eating Chinese food, while Henry told elaborate stories about her and exaggerated them all. Nash had rolled up his sleeves, and Freya found herself relaxing. This was the man she chatted with at night. The man who teased her and let her call him Ignatius. This was the man she had been slowly falling in love with for the past few months. She had missed him.

Henry cleared up the mess. "I'm going to retire for the night. I'll be just down the hall."

Freya watched his retreating back. Then she turned to Nash. "This was nice. Thank you."

Nash followed her into the living room. "I like your grandpa."

Freya took a seat. "Yeah, me too."

Nash took a seat beside her. "You didn't mention him during our calls."

Freya scooted closer to him. "I didn't want to bring up any bad memories."

Nash traced the line of her jaw with his finger. "I don't mind talking about my grandfather. We were close. Like you are with yours. My biggest regret is that we didn't get to know each other as adults."

Freya found herself with her legs draped over Nash's lap, his hands around her hips. She leaned into him. She touched the gold locket she wore around her neck. "I don't know what I'd do without him. He's the only family I have."

Nash leaned back against the couch, content to hold her. "What happened to your parents?"

Freya touched the skin where he'd unbuttoned the top buttons of his shirt. "They left me with Grandpa and Grandma one day and didn't come back. I was young, and I remember my grandma telling me they were in heaven. When I got older, I learned they had been in a terrible accident. My father was a mountain guide, and my mom would often join him. He and my mom had taken a group out, and a storm hit. There was a rockslide. My parents were killed, along with two others."

Nash touched the gold locket she wore. "And this?"

She laid her fingers over his. "I like to wear it sometimes when I want to feel closer to them. Grandma gave me the locket and said they were watching over me, and this would make sure I never forget them."

Nash turned her face to his. "I'm sorry about your parents."

She brushed a lock of hair off his forehead. "I'm sorry about your grandfather."

Freya didn't protest when Nash's mouth found hers. The soft kisses were punctuated with soft sighs. The kisses were sweet, exploratory. Her hand slipped further inside his shirt, unbuttoning a few more buttons so she could explore his chest. She shivered when she felt his fingers stroking the outside of her thigh where her skirt had ridden up.

In mutual agreement, he deepened the kiss and twisted until she lay under him on the sofa. She felt his thigh slide between hers and his fingers curl over her backside, slipping under the waistband of her underwear. She yanked his shirt out of his slacks and shaped the muscles of his back under her palms. Desire coiled in her belly. She arched under him, her mouth blindly seeking his.

The open-mouthed kiss was the most erotic kiss she'd ever experienced. She writhed and whimpered under the weight of him as his fingers found her core and stroked her. Memories of the last time they lay together like this came to the fore.

Nash's breath was warm against her ear. "We can't do this, Freya. Henry is down the hall. But let me do it this way. I owe you one, after all."

The reminder that Henry was down the hall was not a welcome one. But he was right. They couldn't make love on the sofa, and it didn't feel right to take him to her bed. She started to pull away, but his mouth closed over hers again, and his finger stroked deep inside. She clamped her thighs together, but that didn't stop him.

Nash's voice was rough in her ear. "Open for me, sweetheart."

Unable to resist, she opened her thighs to him as he stroked her again. She buried her face in his shoulder to stifle the noises she knew she was making. This time he didn't withdraw, and before she knew it, she convulsed in his arms.

Nash withdrew his fingers and pulled her skirt back into place. He kissed her brow and held her. His voice was rough in her ear. "God, you're beautiful. Next time we eat Chinese at my house."

"Nash?" She pulled her head out of his neck so she could

see his face.

Nash kissed her and settled her back on the sofa. He stood to button his shirt. "I should go."

Despite her muscles feeling like putty and her insides still quivering from the orgasm he'd given her, she couldn't help but look at the fly of his slacks.

Nash's smoky eyes held hers. "Next time, Freya. I'll call you when I get home."

Freya remained limp on the couch and watched him leave. It was several minutes before she was sure her legs would hold her. She locked the front door, grabbed her purse, and went to bed to wait for Nash's call.

He didn't disappoint. She answered her phone on the first ring. "Hello, Ignatius."

Nash's chuckle came over the line. "You're the only woman I've met who can make my full name sound sexy when she says it. Of course, you're the only woman I've told my full name to."

Freya snuggled under the covers and felt her body relax. "You know, when I was getting ready for our date, I distinctly remember thinking that you weren't going to see my underwear."

Nash's voice came back over the line. "To be fair, I didn't actually see your underwear. I only touched them. Can I see you tomorrow?"

Freya closed her eyes. "I have to work for the next five days."

"Friday. I'll pick you up after work."

They chatted a little longer before Freya's voice started to fade. He wished her good night.

* * *

Nash set the phone on the nightstand. He closed his eyes and savored the vision of Freya in his arms. She had been so soft, so responsive. This time he'd been in control of himself. At dinner tonight, he realized he'd approached their date all wrong. He'd treated her like he would have any other date. But now he knew better. She didn't need the Nash he showed the world. She needed the one he kept inside. The one that came out only with those he cared about.

Freya was everything he had imagined and more. These past few weeks she'd kept her distance. And he couldn't blame her. But tonight she'd been heaven in his arms. If he had any sense, he'd stay away from her. He wasn't looking for love and marriage. Gideon was right; he was afraid. The thought of marriage frightened him. He didn't know if he had that kind of love inside of him. Despite all that, despite knowing Freya deserved more from him than a casual relationship, the only thing that had kept him from making love to her again was Henry down the hall.

Nash climbed out of bed, too restless to sleep now that he'd spoken to Freya. He went to his closet and pulled down a box. He set the lid aside. The article about his grandfather's murder lay on top. Cormac's beloved face looked up at him, a face that looked so much like his own.

He set that aside and pulled out the next picture. Maggie. He had loved her so much. They'd been so young, and they'd clung to each other like the two lost souls they were. She had lost her mother when she had been a child and had been raised by her step-father. He had abused her from the time she was fourteen until she'd run away at sixteen.

They'd both been nineteen when they met. He was already growing bored with modeling and traveling. The only reason he stuck with it was that Trenton often joined him, and the idea of going home held little appeal. Trenton had his own demons to battle, and Nash knew Trenton needed to get away, to find a way to live with what ate him up inside. Nash knew because that's what he had been doing.

Maggie had been doing the same. Modeling kept them afloat. Nash was sought after in Europe, and he worked steadily for the first six months. He and Maggie had at first fallen into a casual relationship that quickly became serious. He never told Maggie what had happened to him; he couldn't burden her with it. But being with her, seeing her happy, had made him happy. They had talked about getting married, living in Paris, and spending the rest of their days doing anything and everything they could dream of.

The day Maggie overdosed and died was the day that dream ended. He hadn't been enough for her to overcome her demons. He quit modeling and had come home. To try to drown the agony losing her caused, he had thrown himself into Camhion Enterprises. His father had tried to help him. He worked with his father, and while he loved his father, he hated the work. In an attempt to get his head on straight, he'd left for six months. The backbreaking labor and the hours he'd spent on an oil rig had allowed him to beat the frustration, pain, and suffering out of him. He'd come home and found a way to come to grips with all that life had thrown at him. To appease his dad, he had gone back to school and gotten the law degree he didn't want. He'd gone back to the desk job for a few years. But he was going crazy behind that desk. His father saw it and did what Nash hadn't the heart to do. He fired his son.

He glanced back at his phone. He didn't have a picture of Freya. Not that he needed one. Her face had been haunting his dreams for weeks. They texted most nights. After she had come the day of Cantwell's launch and had agreed to come to Gideon's party, he'd taken to calling her in the evenings again. He loved hearing her smoky voice, telling him about her day or answering his questions about her progress on the case.

But tonight he had set that aside. And so had she. They were just two normal adults who were attracted to each other. They'd talked about silly things. He'd enjoyed watching her blush as Henry told stories about her as a child. He could picture a younger version of Freya, all curiosity and spunk. He'd seen hints of it in the adult version.

Nash climbed back into bed, his body aching. It was going to be a long five days.

Chapter Eight

Freya stepped into the hospital room carrying an orchid plant. They were Donna's favorite. Her apartment was filled with lush orchid plants and ferns. She set it down as she checked her friend's color.

"You're looking much better."

Donna's head turned to admire the plant. "I feel better. My head has stopped feeling like little men are jackhammering inside of it. Now it feels like men with normal hammers."

Freya took a seat. She stopped in at least once a day, usually before her shift. The doctors wanted to keep her a couple more days, but she could tell Donna was ready to get out. "How are your parents doing?"

"Less freaked out. I thought Mom was going to have a heart attack. Dad took it a little better, but not much. He might be a cop, but he says he's my dad first. First time I've been injured, and it wasn't even while working."

"I hear your boss is putting you on leave."

Donna grunted at that. "Standard procedure or some such nonsense. He refuses to tell me anything. My partner is still working on it from his desk. Not that either of us found much. More and more dead ends."

"I'm not having much luck either. We've nothing to go on. No way of narrowing down the suspect pool. A fifty-something white male just doesn't cut it."

"So what about a thirty-something white male? How was your date?"

Freya had been bursting to tell her. But Donna hadn't been up to hearing the details. But today she looked so much better. "We had dinner. He took me to a ridiculously expensive restaurant; I embarrassed myself, he bought Chinese food that we ate with Grandpa Henry, and then we made out on the couch. We're seeing each other again on Friday."

"I suppose it is hard to conduct an affair on your grandpa's couch. Friday you'll have to tell me how it goes."

"It sort of already went."

Donna used the bed remote to raise her head. "Excuse me? My dearest Freya, tell me he ravished you."

Freya giggled. She slapped a hand over her mouth. "Wow. I don't know where that came from. I'm a grown woman. A mature one who can handle an affair with the sexiest man I've ever met."

Donna waved that off. "Mature woman or not, I want details."

Freya glanced at the open door, then scooted closer. "He took matters into his own hands, so to speak. It was amazing."

Donna took her friend's hand, her eyes drooping a little. "I'm happy for you. Really happy. He's the luckiest guy. I hope he knows it."

Freya pulled the blanket up to Donna's chin. "No doubt as soon as you're feeling better, you'll tell him how lucky he is."

Donna's lips curled. "Got that right. Now I need to find one. He doesn't have a brother, does he?"

Freya patted her hand. "You already know he doesn't. Besides, aren't you in love with that guy you met a few weeks ago?"

Donna's eyes opened. "No. He was nice, but no spark. I haven't told you this. It's a secret."

Freya continued to pat her hand. "What secret?"

"I'm in love with Brian."

Freya's spine straightened. "Brian as in Agent Lorenzo? Your partner, Brian?"

Donna frowned. "Yeah. I loved him before he was shot and ended up in that wheelchair. We weren't partners then. We had gone out a couple of times, but he didn't seem that into me. When he came back to work, he was assigned as my new partner. He seems to like it just fine."

Freya didn't know what to say. "Has he been by to see you?"

Donna wiped a tear. "He came last night. First time. He's called a lot to check on me. He didn't stay long."

"Oh, sweetie. I had no idea. You're always talking about the different men you go out with. You seem to have a good time."

"I do. But they're not Brian. It's been six months since I let a guy take me home."

That did surprise Freya. Donna was the outgoing one. A lot of men found the badge sexy. Donna didn't seem to mind. She always had a boyfriend, sometimes two. Six months was a long time for Donna. "Have you told him?"

Donna closed her eyes. "No. What's the point? I just

need to get over it. But for now, I'll live vicariously. Saturday, I want details. Now go to work and let me rest."

Freya gave Donna a quick hug and grabbed her bag. She had work to do if she was going to solve this case.

* * *

The urge to visit his dad was strong the next morning. Nash spent the morning going through emails, following the latest comments on the game, and watching the sales numbers rise. He was bursting with so many ideas, but he'd promised Lilah that she could take the next two weeks off before he put her back to work.

So he'd called his driver and headed to Camhion Enterprises. There was a board meeting today, which meant his dad would be at the office. It was rare these days, but he couldn't stay completely away.

"Well, hello, Brother." Penny came around the corner and saw him heading her way.

He kissed her on the cheek when she hugged him. "Thought I'd pop in and say hello. I know Dad's here somewhere."

"Chatting it up with his friends. I should warn you, though. One of them is Hayden."

Nash rolled his shoulders. "Thanks for the warning."

Penny put her arm around him. "Come on, Nash. Everyone deserves a second chance. He's been working really hard."

Nash didn't comment. Penny would forgive almost anything. "Let's go say hello."

Most of the men in the room were his father's age. He recognized all of them. His father's circle of friends hadn't changed much since college. Nash was greeted with hearty handshakes, some slaps on the back, along with admonishments about when he was going to take over Camhion.

Nash laid a hand on Penny's shoulder. "Camhion Enterprises is already under the best Camhion for the job."

Penny was used to the comments, and while her smile was tight, it held. "Sorry, boys, you're stuck with me. Nash is into games these days."

Ansel Reddick nodded at Nash. He was his father's oldest friend. "I hear your company, Cantwell, has hit the gaming world by storm. I had no doubt you'd make a success of whatever you did. I'm sure my grandkids are already playing it. My youngest son, Denton, has twin boys who are now ten."

Nash nodded politely. He and Denton hadn't gotten along. He'd been forced to play with him when Denton and his dad visited. "It's been a while since I've seen him. How about your older son? Gregory?"

A dark-haired man turned at the sound of his name. "Yes?"

Ansel put a hand on the man's shoulder. "My oldest son, Gregory. He's just moved back to town permanently. He worked for a national firm but finally decided to give his old man a break and take over my firm."

Nash shook his hand. Gregory was a couple of inches shorter than he was, and about ten years older. "I'm sorry, I don't remember you."

The man smiled, showing his capped teeth. "I stayed with my mother a lot."

Ansel's mouth tightened. "Divorce is never easy. But Denton's mother and I are still married and going on forty-five years, same as your old man."

Penny squeezed Nash's shoulder. "I'll let you men catch up. See you later, Dad."

Eldridge kissed his daughter on the cheek. "I'll stop in before I go. And I want to check in on Levi."

"Best guy on the team." Penny left the room.

Nash wished he could go with him, but part of his role in the family was dealing with Dad's friends so Penny didn't have to.

Hayden joined the group. "Hello, Nash."

Nash glanced at him but didn't respond. He turned back to Gregory. "What sort of work did you do before?"

Gregory gestured vaguely. "Couldn't seem to settle in one place. Did a little bit of everything."

Ansel gripped his son's shoulder. "He's modest. He taught business seminars all over the country. He always had a head for business. Running a construction firm didn't seem glamourous. Denton runs my legal department now. And Gregory oversees all the building projects. We were just showing your dad the specs on our latest build. Make a good piece of real estate for Camhion Enterprises."

Nash couldn't have cared less. "I'll let you dazzle Penny. Are you all heading to lunch?"

Gregory glanced at his watch. "Actually, we have a lunch appointment. And I do want to try to dazzle your sister. It's an excellent property, and we could come to terms on additional work."

Nash held the door for the group as the other men all made excuses to leave. "Well, then, we'll catch up some other time. Dad, I'll join you."

Nash sighed in relief when the group of men left. Hayden excused himself. "The deal any good?"

Eldridge nodded. "It's a good property. Penny has the numbers. She plans to inspect it herself. Ansel knows what he's doing. It's a shame, though. Gregory doesn't have the talent his father has. Ansel still controls the day to day. And Denton, well, he gets paid and that's all he cares about."

Nash stopped his dad. Guilt had been gnawing at him. "I need to talk to you. It's important."

The men slipped into a nearby office. Eldridge crossed his arms protectively across his chest. "The only time you take that tone is when it's about your grandfather."

Nash closed the door and leaned against it. "I didn't want to say anything before. You and Mom were on your trip. And nothing has changed. But I haven't been honest with you. Freya, from the party the other night, is working in partnership with the FBI. An agent contacted me about some new evidence."

Eldridge sat, the color draining from his face. "What evidence?"

Nash slipped into the chair next to him. "DNA."

Eldridge growled. "The only DNA found on your grandfather was his own. And a few fibers that could have come from anywhere."

Nash clasped his hands between his knees. "There was evidence collected at the hospital on me."

Eldridge was confused. "The blood on you was yours."

Nash held his father's eyes. "There was DNA on me. His DNA. A semen sample was taken at the scene."

Eldridge lost what little color he had left. "But the doctors said…"

Nash took his father's cold hand. "He didn't. But it was there all the same. I don't remember when they swabbed it."

Eldridge's hand gripped his son's. "You weren't talking. Your mother and I waited in the hallway while you changed. Why didn't you tell me?"

Nash squeezed and let his father's hand go. "I couldn't tell you. I couldn't tell anyone. I didn't tell the doctors or the therapist. I didn't know how to process it. God, Dad, I was thirteen. I was just getting interested in girls, so I wasn't totally ignorant about what was happening. But I was horrified; disgusted when you come right down to it. I felt like what happened was something I had done. That I had done something that caused him to assault me. I was messed up for a long time."

Eldridge leaned in and took his son in his arms. "You should have told me."

Nash let his dad hold him for a moment before he pulled away and shrugged. "The evidence was lost, and as far as Gideon can tell, its collection wasn't in any of the reports. So you wouldn't have known it existed. Freya was digging into the files and wanted to look at some of the evidence from Grandfather's murder when she came upon a box with my name on it. She said it was pushed behind his evidence boxes. So she ran it. It was tied to other kidnappings. The kids didn't survive."

Eldridge took a moment to compose himself. "They know who he is?"

Nash stood and started pacing. He hated seeing that flicker of hope in his dad's eyes. And being the one to crush it. "No, Dad. Just a profile. Freya found a hit here in D.C. from a murder last year with the same DNA. It's tied to a series of murders across the country. This guy has been doing this a long time. And he's still at it."

Eldridge rose and stood so Nash had to stop his pacing. "What did the FBI say?"

"That I was likely the first. That Grandfather's murder was unique for this guy. She didn't spell it out, but I think she thinks we know who it was. Why kill Grandfather?"

"We always thought it had to be a stranger. We didn't want to believe someone we knew would do this to us. Every person we knew back then was questioned. Background checks were run. Some people submitted to polygraphs. We lost a lot of friends during that time. Hayden stayed by my side. Most of the men in that boardroom today did, too. If it weren't for Hayden and Ansel, a few of the deals that were in the works would have collapsed, and Camhion Enterprises would have gone with them."

Had Camhion Enterprises collapsed, Nash wasn't sure his father would be with them today. His father had sought refuge in his work many times over the years. His parents' marriage had suffered. But somehow, they had all come through those dark days. Nash hated dredging this up, but when Cantwell wasn't consuming him, this case was. He'd gotten a text from Freya that she wanted him to come to the precinct and look over knives with her.

What if this man had gone after Freya, other than knocking her down? What if he came back? He knew Agent Monaco was out of intensive care and was likely to be released any day. What if he sought Freya out?

Eldridge interrupted his thoughts. His voice was hoarse from the emotions he was holding in. "I can't believe there are more murders. That he is still out there. We never thought beyond what happened to us. Does the FBI need to chat with me and your mother?"

Nash knew his words would hurt. "I told them not to."

"Nash? What did you do?"

Nash resumed his pacing when his father stepped out of his way. "You and Mom were on your trip. They don't have anything new. But Gideon is working on the latest murder, and Freya is helping the FBI. I didn't want to rock the boat. I told Penny some of the details, but she learned the rest a few days ago."

Eldridge grabbed his arm. "He was my father, Nash. You're my son. It's my job to protect you. Not the other way around."

"I know."

Eldridge continued. "So why tell me now?"

Nash turned troubled gray eyes to his father. "Freya. Agent Donna Monaco, the FBI agent, is a friend of Freya's. They were out at lunch and Donna was attacked. She's been in the ICU. The attacker confronted Freya. He had a knife, but he didn't use it on her. But he showed it to her, like it was some sort of damn trophy. Gideon thinks it was our man. And so do I. I feel it."

"And what of Freya? Your tone changes when you say her name."

And wasn't that the crux of his problem? "I don't want to love her."

Eldridge's body language changed from anger to understanding. "You've lost a lot, son. We didn't know Maggie, but her death tore open all the wounds that still hadn't healed. I could tell when we met Freya that you care about her. Your mother commented on it on the way home."

Nash took a deep breath and slowly let it out. "I don't know what to do. I don't know what I feel."

Eldridge smiled. "Women are the greatest mystery. I've been married to your mother for forty-five years and I still don't always know what to do. But I will tell you that there is nothing I would not do for her. I'd die for her. I'd die for you and Penny."

Nash knew his father meant every word. "Just don't get your hopes up about Grandfather. Gideon has been trying to solve this for years."

"I have faith in Gideon. And so do you. And it seems you have faith in Freya. We won't tell your mother or your grandmother yet. We'll wait and see. But Nash?"

Nash stopped pacing. "Yeah?"

"Keep me in the loop this time."

Nash pulled open the conference room door. "I will."

* * *

Nash figured some promises were easier to keep than

others. He didn't tell Penny about his conversation with their dad. No doubt Eldridge called Gideon the moment he left Camhion. Which meant that Penny knew he had told their dad; Gideon would have told her. The longer he had kept it from his father, the worse his guilt had gotten. And if the man who attacked Agent Monaco was his attacker, it was better that his father knew this man was still out there. A feeling of dread was hovering, and Nash couldn't shake it.

His driver dropped him off at the precinct. He'd texted Freya, and she had told him that now was a good time. And it was Friday.

She greeted him within minutes of his arrival. "Hi. I hope you weren't busy."

Nash wanted to grab and kiss her, but he simply tucked his hands into his trouser pockets. "I took the day off. I spent the morning at the gym, then I hung out at Camhion Enterprises for a little while. Stakeholder meeting today. Dad was there, so I dropped in. I like to make an appearance for his friends once in a while."

Freya gave him an odd glance. "I would think you'd see them a lot; you being the heir and all."

He hated that phrase. "Not me. Penny. Penny is happy when I keep my nose out of it. But I made a promise years ago that I'd be the dutiful son. Dad's satisfied with me showing up at parties now and again, popping into investor meetings, and staying on top of the business."

Freya guided him to her office. The room was tiny and meticulously organized. "I see the pictures. You do your fair share. And the ladies love you."

Nash dropped into the seat opposite her. "Is that a hint

of jealousy?"

Freya tipped her head; her eyes narrowed. "Maybe."

Nash lay on the charm. He took her hand and kissed it. "You flatter me."

She giggled, but then her eyes turned serious. "There isn't another woman, is there? I mean, I'm not sure what exactly is happening between us, but given what we plan to do tonight, I'd like to know."

She was serious. He tried to find the right words. "There hasn't been a woman in a while. There has been barely time to breathe. First, there was Penny and my crazed cousin. Then Ginny and Trenton. And then that mess with Isaac. Cantwell has been a whirlwind. And the truth is, there was something between us before we even met. I don't know what is happening either. And I can't make promises, Freya. But there are no other women."

"Okay."

The one-word response threw him. "This is where you say there are no other men."

"Oh, right. No other men."

She looked like she wanted to say something else, but she instead cleared her throat and pulled a tablet out of her desk.

"I've not made a lot of progress as far as familial DNA. I can tell you he's white, and the DNA profile says he's brunette. But nothing we don't already know. Gideon would know more about the ongoing investigation on the FBI side. But Gideon drew the knife I saw right after Donna's attack. I did some research. I don't know how much you remember, but I wanted you to look at some pictures to see if any of these knives look familiar."

His gut clenched, but he took the tablet. She looked apologetic but determined. He could appreciate her determination. The first picture was a sketch. "Gideon drew this. I can tell."

"From my description. I learned more about knives and metal the past couple of days than I ever wanted to. I couldn't find one exactly like the one I saw. But I think I can make a composite one using different pictures. But I wanted you to look at them first."

Nash slowly scrolled through the pictures. Flashes came and went. He held out his hands about a foot and a half apart. "It was about this long. It was substantial, like a hunting knife. I was drugged, so I can't be sure. It looked huge."

She scrolled to the next. "These are various metals."

Nash closed his eyes. "It wasn't shiny, but light did reflect off it. It wasn't like anything I had seen before. It almost looked like stone."

Freya moved to the next set of images. "Like this?"

Nash froze. "Like stone."

"Damascus steel. Its look is unique. This particular knife is handmade."

Nash pointed to one. "This one."

Freya kept going. "Handles. I didn't get as good a look at it."

Nash scrolled through a few. "Not plastic. His hand was holding it most of the time, but I do know that. It was a lighter color. Maybe like these bone handles. Or maybe antlers."

Freya turned to her computer. She worked for a few. "Anything else?"

"Gold."

She stopped. "Gold?"

"Bottom of the knife. It had a gold base; I don't know, like a cap on the end. I remember it. Flashed like a gold watch. It was like being hypnotized, the flash of light, the glint on the metal. It also had two gold bands at the top of the hilt. Just kept flashing."

Freya went back to her computer. Ten minutes later, she turned her screen. "Does this look like what you saw?"

Nash swore. "That's damn close."

Freya turned the screen back and took the tablet back. "I don't know if it will help. But I can start doing some searches."

Nash swallowed and willed himself to relax. "Like comparing knife sales to people we knew back then?"

"Can't hurt. Maybe someone was a collector. This is not exactly distinct, but it's not your run-of-the-mill military weapon or average hunter's weapon, either. Would be much easier if it were some weird ceremonial piece or something. Or an antique."

Nash watched Freya as she typed. "How is your friend? Home?"

"Yes. She's home. Today, actually. Her parents are with her. I think her dad is trying to convince her to come with them for a little while. At least until the FBI figures out who attacked her. Her partner is working around the clock, from what I've gathered. I've been in touch with him, but nothing yet."

Gideon had told him the FBI wasn't any closer to an ID than they were the day of her attack. No cameras had picked up more than what Freya saw. "Can we get out of here?"

Freya's hands froze. "Uh, yeah. You were my last meeting today, and my team left an hour ago."

Nash watched as Freya gathered her things. The white polo shirt and navy slacks she wore looked exactly like the ones she'd been wearing the day they met. "Have I told you I find polo shirts sexy?"

Freya fumbled her purse. "What?"

Nash rocked back on his heels. "Very sexy."

"Um, I should probably go home and change for dinner."

Nash took her hand, and he walked them outside. "I know how to order pizza. You could not go home and change, and we could go straight to my house."

Freya's hand shook as she took her keys out of her purse. "I like pizza."

Nash pulled her to a stop next to her car. "Grandpa Henry expecting you home?"

"I told him I was working late. I don't think he believed me. He told me he didn't expect me home until morning. He likes you. He says I need more friends."

Nash pulled her to him. He tucked a strand of hair behind her ear. Her eyes were unsure. "If nothing else, Freya, we are friends. We don't have to go back to my place. We don't have to do anything you don't want to do."

Freya stood on her tiptoes and lightly kissed him. "I've never had a friend like you. And I want to go to your place. I just don't know if I'll be good at them or not, but there are lots of things I'd like to do with you."

Nash pulled away from her tantalizing kiss. "I am so glad you said that. It's been forever."

Freya did the math. "It's been five weeks, Ignatius."

He roughly kissed her before opening her car door. "Exactly. Forever."

Chapter Nine

Freya wasn't exactly sure what to expect. Sex, obviously. Every time they were together, they couldn't keep their hands to themselves. But he didn't seem to be in a hurry.

Nash tossed his wallet and keys on a side table. "Can I get you a drink?"

Freya set her purse next to his wallet. "Just water. It was a long day."

Freya followed him to the kitchen. She took the sparkling water from him.

Nash leaned against the counter, his eyes cloudy as they watched her. "I don't know how you do it. Same for Gideon. I've only seen a small fraction of what the two of you see every day."

Freya had heard that question before. The end result usually was that the man never called again. "I never witnessed a violent crime. I was never a victim. That's what you're really asking me. Gideon did, though now I know it was in the role of rescuer. So what would drive a person to pursue a job where they deal with the worst that humanity has to offer day in and day out?"

Nash didn't move. "I suppose that is the real question."

Freya was never good at articulating the reasons. Her gaze dropped to the tips of her black orthopedic shoes. "I suppose the same thing that drives people to the military, or the medical profession. Or to climb towers, chase storms, fly airplanes, or build skyscrapers. There is something inside that pushes you to find truth, protect others, to save, to preserve, to challenge. Or maybe just to leave the world in better shape when you leave it than it was when you came into it. I don't know."

"I think those are great reasons."

She looked up at him through her lashes. "And I like science."

Nash took her hand. "I've been wanting to show you something."

Freya was confused as he led her up a flight of stairs. "I really thought you meant your bedroom."

Nash bent and kissed the side of her neck. His breath whispered across her skin. "That, too."

Freya looked around in interest. The open room was filled with desks, computers, easels, dry erase boards, and what to her eyes looked like chaos. "Not sure this is how I pictured Cantwell's office."

Nash glanced around and shrugged. "We make it work. My office is back there. I need a quiet space for phone calls. But I wanted to show you the art room."

Nash punched in a code to unlock the door. Freya followed him inside. All the walls were filled with drawings, photos, and story boards. She'd played enough of the game that she recognized some of the artwork. She smiled when she saw the portraits of the four men. She went over for a closer look. "These are great. Lilah did these, right?"

"Yes. Just these alone were worth hiring her for. She

had a huge influence on the game. She brought depth to the men through these that they would have lacked."

She touched the last one. She could see Nash's likeness. "The prince. He's a complex character. They all are."

Nash came up behind her. "That was all Isaac."

She leaned back against him. "I finished the book. It made me cry and made me believe the world could be changed. If you want it bad enough. It made me believe in destiny. In love. In overcoming all obstacles and triumph."

Nash's lips were light in her hair. "I want to show you the others."

Freya's muscles fluttered at the touch of his fingers on her belly as he brought his arm around her. Her breath caught at the portraits of the women. She'd seen them in the game, but to see them here, drawn in pencil and chalk, brought a new depth to them.

"Gideon. His talent is off the charts. Like Isaac. Isaac will say his book is pure imagination. Gideon dreamed these."

"They're beautiful."

Nash came beside her. "One for each."

Something Nash said to her the night of the party nagged at her. "They look like..."

Nash pointed. "Penny. Ginny. Lilah."

Freya put two and two together. She hadn't made the connection before. "Gideon would have drawn these before they even met."

Nash came to stand beside the fourth. "Yes, he did. Isaac will say Gideon drew Penny because he's in love with her, and always has been. He'll say Ginny is coincidence. He hasn't come up with a satisfactory reason for Lilah."

Her eyes captured his. "And the fourth?"

Nash traced her cheek. "Do you believe in fate, Freya?"

Freya turned to the last woman. "In Norse mythology, there were three goddesses of fate: Urd, Verdandi, and Skuld. Grandpa Henry told me they wove the tapestry of fate. He never cursed fate; he said it decreed that his son would be taken from him. He says you can't accept just the good. You have to accept the bad, too. Yes. I believe in fate: divine providence."

Nash turned her to face him. "I don't. But I see you there. When you appeared in the gardens at the hotel, you were like a dream that walked into my life. The hair. The dress. The desire I felt in that moment was more than anything I'd ever experienced. Not lust, Freya. Desire."

She touched the painting. The white dress, the silver ribbon. She'd worn her hair down that night. A rare occurrence. It was uncanny how much she looked like the woman in the painting that night. "This is what your friends meant. What you meant. The woman you're supposed to marry."

"I could have strangled them for it."

She didn't understand. "Then why am I here? You don't believe in fate. You don't believe in dreams. I don't blame you, Ignatius. You lived through something horrific. I know you believe in love, but I can see the shadows inside you that hide it."

Nash took her arms and brought them around his neck. His hands slid down her skin, making her shiver. "You're here because I want to believe. Because I can't seem to find the words to push you away. I loved someone once; it seems like a lifetime ago. I swore I would never love anyone else. You deserve more than I'm willing to give. I told you once to leave. I'm only going to tell you one more time, Freya. If you can't or won't accept limits, you should leave."

Oh, how she wished it were that easy. He didn't see what she saw. "I couldn't leave then. I won't now."

A growl was torn from his throat. He bent, slipped his arms under her legs, and carried her down the stairs.

The moment he dropped her legs, she wound herself around him. Her weight pulled them both down onto the bed. He managed to take most of his weight off her as they landed. Her hands fisted in his gorgeous hair, using the long strands to pull his mouth to hers. Her legs parted to cradle him against her. Her hips lifted in desire as their lips and limbs tangled.

Nash pulled slightly away. His breathing was harsh. "We should slow this down."

Freya didn't want to slow down, but his hands stopped her as she reached for him. He tugged her blouse from her slacks, and his hands went from her hips to her rib cage to her breasts. He smiled at the sight of her sports bra. He removed it with the blouse.

His fingers danced over her skin. "You're so lovely, Freya. Inside and out. These past months you've been a balm. Moments of peace in the whirlwind."

Freya felt tears sting her eyes. "Nash."

His lips took hers once again. His hands were gentle as he peeled away the rest of her clothes. He left no inch of her skin untouched. Now she wanted to touch. He helped her as she removed his clothes. His muscles were sleek under her palms. She pressed her lips wherever they reached as he held her against him.

She pressed her palms to his chest, the soft hair tickling her fingers. "You have the most fantastic chest. Did I tell you that? It's even better now."

Nash groaned as her fingers grazed his nipples. "No, I don't think you did."

She molded all the fantastic muscles as she memorized them with her hands. She kissed his neck as she pressed her breasts against him. "All sleek and sexy."

Nash stroked the length of her back, pressing her every curve to him. He took her hair out of its topknot. "You're so soft. Every inch of you."

Freya twisted so that she was once again on her back. She pulled him to her. "How about you find out how soft I can be?"

Nash swore as he reached for a condom in the nightstand. He rolled it on and settled between her thighs. Without another word, he lifted her hips and pressed inside.

She gasped at the full feeling of him inside her. Like last time, she held him, her nails digging into his back. With each stroke, she followed, her mind shutting off as her body took over. She was keenly aware of the press of his belly to hers. The way his skin slid against hers as he moved inside. His arms were under her back, his lips in her hair. She heard herself calling his name. He heard her pleas. He shifted, angling her hips as he slid even deeper. Breath caught; she convulsed around him.

Nash held her, his voice hoarse in her ear. "Again."

She was still dazed, or she might have protested. But his pace increased, and she held on as he took her over the edge again. She was dimly aware of his climax before he collapsed onto her.

She thought she might have dozed. Nash roused her as he withdrew. This time he tossed the condom in a trash bin near the bed and gathered her against him. She laid her head on his chest as he held her. His heart rate was slowing as they both relaxed. She smoothed her palm over his chest, her fingers enjoying the softness of his skin.

Her fingers stilled. She shifted so that she could see his face as she rested on his chest. She smiled at him.

Nash lifted so he could kiss her. "What's with the smile?"

"I really do like your chest."

Nash pulled her closer. "Then it's all yours."

Freya tucked her head to his shoulder, getting comfortable. "Can I ask you a question? You don't have to answer it."

Nash tucked a strand of her hair behind her ear. "I think I might know what it is."

Freya turned her hazel eyes to his. "Who was she?"

Nash released the breath he'd held. "Yeah. That's what I thought you were going to ask. Her name was Maggie. I was in France. We met. We fell in love. She died."

"Oh, Nash. I'm so sorry. I shouldn't have asked."

He kissed away her apology. "I was nineteen when I met her. She was a lot like me, and I guess I felt like she could understand what was inside me. She had lost her mom and had been abused by her step-father. I never told her what was done to me; I didn't have to. I don't think she wanted to hear it. But she knew. We were together for a couple of years. I was working a lot, and I didn't notice things had gotten worse with her. I didn't understand why she was depressed one moment and euphoric the next. I was so naïve."

Freya sat up, taking the sheet with her, covering her breasts. "She was doing drugs."

Nash scrubbed his face with his palms. "Yeah. I was drinking too much. Alcohol was my vice of choice when the memories were too much. She found pills. One day, she took them all. She left me a note."

Freya had read a few herself over the years. Proving authenticity. Too often the words were very real. "That's when you stopped modeling."

The surprise on his face was real. "You know about that?"

She nodded. "I still have a magazine with you on it. And your fantastic chest. It's improved with age."

Nash laughed. He looked surprised by it. "Freya, your effect on me amazes me. Yeah, that's when I stopped modeling and put my shirt back on. It was a rough couple of years. Isaac was away; turns out he was working at the Pentagon. Gideon was a fresh cop. He was already digging into my grandfather's murder and my kidnapping back then. Trenton was making his first million. Then his second, third, and so on. I spent six months on an oil rig. Best and worst six months of my life. I figured I had two choices: end up like Maggie or get my life together. Gideon, Isaac, and Trenton gave me something to live for. My parents and Penny, too. Dad kept me working until I was ready to strike out on my own."

Freya stretched out beside him. "What was she like?"

Nash stared at the ceiling. "She was tall and slim. Her hair was raven black and fell to her waist. Her eyes were electric blue. As a fanciful young man, I swore she'd put a spell on me. Honestly, outside of bed, we didn't have much in common. She wrote dark poetry and spent a lot of her time in underground clubs with like-minded people. In hindsight, I realized she embraced the darker side of life. But that's where I was then."

Freya could only think of how damaged Maggie must have been. She could feel pity for the young woman who wasn't able to find her way out of the darkness she had lived. Freya cupped Nash's cheek and kissed him. Her lips molded to his, hoping her presence made the memories a little easier.

Nash didn't kiss her back. "Aren't you going to ask me about myself?"

Freya leaned back and released the sheet. She brought his hands to her breasts. "No. I'm not going to ask. And you don't have to tell me, Nash. I don't want your secrets if you don't want me to have them."

His fingers molded her nipples as he sat up and replaced his hands with his mouth. He suckled at her as one of his hands strayed between her thighs. She wasn't sure what she thought she'd accomplish, but her own arousal took her by surprise. He took his time with her, and she let him do with her what he would; she wholeheartedly offered herself to him. When he was once again buried inside her, she held him as tears fell.

Spent both physically and emotionally, they slept.

* * *

Nash was whistling in the kitchen as he cooked breakfast. He was an early riser, and he could tell from the dark circles under Freya's eyes that she was working too hard. He left her sleeping.

He heard the front door open and knew who was at the door. "In the kitchen, Gideon."

Gideon peeked around the corner. "I saw Freya's car outside."

Nash's brow rose at that. "So you thought, hey, I should go over there?"

Gideon came in and poured a cup of coffee. "Figured I'd chance it. If you were both in here naked, I'd have left."

Nash took a sip of his coffee. "You almost sounded like Trenton there for a second."

Gideon grimaced. "He does wear off on you."

Nash scraped the scrambled eggs onto a plate. He grabbed the toast. "Here. I know you haven't eaten yet. Freya will probably sleep a while longer."

Gideon took a seat and accepted the plate. "Thanks. You're not as good as Isaac, but you're a million times better than I am in the kitchen."

Nash smiled at that. His mother had taught both her kids to cook. For years, all he could manage was a steak. These days, he did a sight better. "I don't know how you and Penny don't starve to death. Penny can cook, but she'd rather not."

Gideon tucked his chin down. "We find other ways to satiate our appetites."

"That's so wrong."

Gideon didn't bother hiding his smile. "We eat lots of sandwiches. We get by. She's serious about the baby thing, by the way. So I guess we'll have to figure out something besides sandwiches."

Nash took a seat. "I can't wait to be Uncle Nash. You and Penny will be great parents. Mom can teach the kid to cook."

Gideon finished the eggs and toast. "So, how are you?"

Nash glanced to where the bedroom was. "I could love her, Gideon."

Gideon understood. "Already do."

Nash ran frustrated fingers through his hair. "She seemed to understand when I told her about Maggie."

Gideon drained his coffee. "Did you tell her about him?"

Nash swallowed the lump in his throat, glad he'd only drank coffee. "No. And I won't. She said she doesn't need to know if I don't want to tell her. She would have seen the scars, but she didn't act like she noticed them."

Gideon set his hand on his friend's clenched fist. "She saw the pictures of Marcus Henney. She studies crime scenes and evidence. She already knows. She doesn't need the details. And I'm happy she's not trying to force them from you."

It should bother him. She did know. She didn't need his words. But some part of him was happy she did. That she could know without him having to tell her. "She's still here.

I didn't manage to chase her off. So I guess I'm having a good day."

Gideon got up and poured them both a fresh cup. "FBI has been in contact. It's been quiet as far as our guy is concerned. He hasn't dropped any fresh bodies. The FBI's current stance is that Agent Monaco's attack was not related to this case."

Nash's hand tightened on his cup. "That's crap, and we both know it. Why lie?"

Gideon didn't have the answers. "It's not a cover up. And not lies, per se. The agent's boss is a guy named Callahan. His stance is there isn't enough evidence to point to our guy. There was a case and a guy just released from jail that he thinks is good for it. I haven't talked to Agent Monaco yet. She's off duty and on leave, and her boss says it's not our guy, so procedurally, I can't really ask her. But her best friend could."

And the real reason Gideon had come over. Or one of them, anyway. "I can ask Freya. I was planning on spending the day with her. I'm sure a visit to her friend could be on the schedule."

Gideon rose. "You were whistling when I came in."

Nash froze. "So?"

Gideon zipped up his jacket. "Nothing. It was nice. A little rusty, maybe. Haven't heard you do that in a long time."

Nash watched as Gideon left. And he was right; he couldn't remember the last time he whistled. Isaac had told him more than once over the years that a little happiness wouldn't hurt. Up until Gideon married Penny, Isaac said it to both of them. Said he never saw two people happier in their misery. Nash liked to think of it as happy in his heartache. But he got the point.

Nash went about fixing a second breakfast. When he heard stirring down the hall, he cracked a couple more eggs and poured a cup of coffee. He didn't know much about her, but he knew she loved coffee. Black. Just like him.

She came into the kitchen wearing her clothes from yesterday. Her hair was disheveled, and he was pleased she hadn't tied it back up yet. He liked the way it flowed around her shoulders. He handed her the cup.

She thanked him. "How long have you been awake?"

Nash glanced at the clock. It was a little after eight. "Couple of hours. I'm an early riser."

She yawned and took a seat. "My schedule is chaotic, depending on what I'm working on. I just sleep whenever. But you should have woken me up."

Nash came over, leaned down, and kissed her. He didn't make it brief. "You looked peaceful sleeping naked in my bed."

She blushed. "It's a nice bed."

Nash finished making breakfast. She seemed content to watch. But she just looked at the plate when he set it in front of her. "Don't like eggs?"

She glanced up as if waking from a trance. "Sorry. I'll eat anything. I was thinking."

"Gideon already did that for me today."

She dug in. "It's hard to think of him as Gideon and not Detective Eginhard."

He finished his coffee and ignored his plate of food.

"You'll have to get used to it. You're sleeping with his best friend."

She looked smug. "Yes, I am. But I should be getting home."

Nash shook his head. "It's Saturday. I thought we could spend the day together. But we should go back to your place for a change of clothes."

"What did you want to do?"

Lusty thoughts filled his brain before common sense won out. "Actually, Gideon wanted us to talk to your friend, Donna. Official word from her boss is that her attack is not related to my case, but a different one. Gideon can't ask her, so he asked you to."

"I hate to be the voice of reason, but it could have been someone else."

Nash's gut clenched. "I'd concede it's a possibility if it weren't for the knife you saw."

She couldn't deny that fact. "Maybe I should go by myself."

Nash cleaned up the dishes, tossing the food he didn't eat. "Why? Worried about me hanging out with the FBI agent working on my case?"

She cleared her throat. "Not exactly, though it's a concern. You were pretty mad at me. And in turn, Donna."

"And now I'm not. So it's not a problem."

She bit her bottom lip. "She might ask some personal questions you might not want to answer. Like if you were able to sexually satisfy her friend."

That gave him pause. "Never thought of myself as the topic of girl talk. Though I'd love to hear how I measured up."

She rose from her seat as he came toward her. She took a step back. "I think you know the answer to that question."

He scooped her up. "A man loves to hear the words."

She giggled the entire way to the bedroom.

* * *

"I didn't think you two would show up." Donna waved at them from where she was resting on her couch.

Freya closed the door behind them. Nash had his hands tucked in his pockets, and his expression was closed. He didn't look mad, not exactly. But he didn't look thrilled either.

"I hope you don't mind us popping in."

Donna adjusted the back of her recliner, so she was sitting. "My parents left this morning. My mom is satisfied I'm not dying. My dad, well, he'll go down and find my boss and rip into him until he gets the answers he wants."

Freya took a seat and patted at the spot beside her for Nash to do the same. "Your dad is scary when he's mad. I wouldn't want to be your boss right now."

Donna grimaced. "More like a dog with an old bone. Or an old dog with an old bone. SSA Callahan will survive. But that's not why you're here. You said something about my attacker on the phone."

Nash stayed silent, so Freya continued. "Well, Detective Eginhard stopped by this morning to talk to Nash. He said the official line is that your attack is not related to the murder of Marcus Henny. Or the Camhion cases."

"Luther Rodriguez got out of jail two days before my attack. A particularly nasty specimen of humanity. Got out on a technicality. I'm still torqued the that judge allowed it. He'll be retried, and if justice prevails, he'll be back in jail by the end of the year. But it was my eyewitness account that clinched the original case. When it goes back to trial, my testimony will land him right back in jail."

"He would definitely be a contender."

Donna shrugged. "Likely he'll skip the country. He's got tight criminal ties with some folks in South America. But you said that in the past tense."

Freya glanced at Nash. He simply nodded at her. "Nash recognized the knife. I sent the file to Gideon, and he'll pass it along."

Donna's eyes focused. "Traceable?"

"Don't know. But that's my next task tomorrow."

Donna closed her eyes. "Surprised you aren't there now."

Nash's response was a light snort.

Donna perked up. "Oh. Right. So how did it go?"

Freya knew her face was bright red. She knew Donna wouldn't hesitate to ask in front of Nash. "Very well, thank you."

Donna's laugh was contagious. "You should see your face right now. But I'm glad. I'm not up to punching anyone out today."

"Speaking of, has Brian stopped by?"

Donna glanced at the oversized clock over her television. "He said he'll stop by this afternoon. He's promised to catch me up. He's been looking into Rodriguez, but I think we both know he's not going to find anything. Likely Brian already interrogated him. Callahan would have had him picked up. But Brian did speak with Detective Eginhard this morning. So he'll get the file on the knife as well. Marcus Henney was just a normal fourteen-year-old. He liked sports and played basketball. He loved English literature. He was an honor student. Top of his class at The Leighton Academy."

"Wait? What?" Nash's interest perked. "Gideon didn't mention the school."

Freya shifted to face him. "So? What's the significance?"

"It's a private school. A very exclusive, very expensive private school. I know people who went there."

Donna groaned as she got to her feet, but she was steady as she went and grabbed her laptop. "Let me see. Wasn't your school. And the other D.C. victim, the second one, was enrolled at a different school than both you and Marcus. Damn, a Catholic private school. Pricey, too. The victim was twelve. Not rich."

Freya came up behind her. "He was there on a scholarship program. Top of his class."

Twenty minutes later, Donna was swearing. "Every victim was in a private school, top of his class. We took the information down, and we cross-referenced victims, but the system didn't distinguish public versus private. Nash, I'm guessing you were an honor student."

Freya watched as Nash took deep breaths, forcing the emotions back. "Isaac was valedictorian. I was salutatorian. I was good at school. And I was competitive and always trying to best Isaac. Never happened, of course. Then after the attack, school gave me something to focus on."

Freya pulled her tablet out of her purse. "We know all the victims have superficial traits that match. Dark hair color, height, and age. Finding gray-eyed kids in a private school would be nearly impossible. I researched it. Only three percent of the population has gray eyes. Eye color was usually brown, but he wasn't faithful to it. Overachieving private school students. Seems extremely specific."

Nash tucked his hands between his knees. "How about uniforms?"

Freya scrolled through her files. "Not all. Marcus was wearing one. But not all were snatched at school."

Donna set her laptop down. "School security has tightened over the years. Cameras, police officers, metal detectors, you name it. Schools can go on lockdown fast. Marcus was grabbed outside a restaurant where he was hanging out with some friends. But it was right after school. His mom was in the car; she saw the whole thing. Coincidentally, reading it again, it matches the description of the man you saw, Freya. He wore a black face mask, a Washington Capitals baseball cap, brown hair, and average height. Tan jacket, though. But otherwise, it sounds like our guy."

Nash got up and started pacing. "So what does it say about a man who cuts and murders teenage boys who are honor students at private schools?"

Freya considered it. "Well, it could be himself. Sometimes serial killers try to destroy themselves. He could have seen himself in you. Or they could be surrogates for his real target. In this case, you. If we go on the premise that you were the first, each murder has been an attempt to recreate your abduction and finish what he couldn't finish with you."

Nash's hands fisted. "Then how do you reconcile that with my grandfather's murder? Did he hate his dad or something?"

Donna took offense at his tone. "Things only have to make sense to the killer. Don't try to put a rational lens on this guy. He could have hated his dad. He could have resented the relationship he perceived between you and your grandfather. Killing your grandfather may not have given him the same high as you. Think about it. He shot Cormac. He didn't cut and stab him."

Nash turned on her. "You said his murder made my case unique. That his murder could be used to find this guy."

Donna held up her hands. "Or it could simply be coincidence. It doesn't feel that way. But it was more like an execution. No pleasure in it for a man who likes to cut."

Freya came up to him and wrapped her arms around him. "Your grandfather is a piece. An important piece. Why you? Cormac being your grandfather might be part of the reason why he chose you."

Nash rested his forehead on hers. "I hate this. All we've done for years is go around in circles."

"And we'll keep going around in them until there are no more. You pull threads until you get to the right one. But if he chooses his victims because they remind him of you, then he knew these things about you, or at least he does now. He knows who your parents are. He knows you went to private school. He knows you live in D.C."

Donna chimed in. "What bothers me is that he knows I'm working on this case. I'm new to it. I haven't interviewed that many people. Did someone tell him I was working the case? Which begs the question, who would he know who could tell him? Has he been following you? If he has, and he was able to identify me, he's either got someone helping him, or he hired someone to investigate anyone around the case."

Nash held Freya. "It worries me that he might know about Freya. About my family. I told my dad what happened to you and Freya, and that you came to interview me. If he'll attack an FBI agent, where would he draw the line? Gideon will keep an eagle eye on Penny. My dad will make sure he and my mother are safe. I know how to take precautions. And I'm not a weak teenager anymore. I almost wish he would come after me."

Freya thumped her fist on his chest. "Don't even think about it."

Nash set her back from him. "Why not use me to draw him out?"

Donna set her hand on Freya's shoulder as she glared at Nash. "You're not a teenage boy anymore. You're not his type."

Nash stood his ground. "And if he thought he had a shot at finishing me off, my age wouldn't matter to him. I'm unfinished business."

Freya shuddered. "I'm calling Gideon."

Freya went to grab her purse, but Nash took it before she could. "Give me my bag, Nash."

"You know I'm right."

Freya pushed him and snatched her purse. "That's what scares me."

Donna held up her phone. "I already texted him."

Freya felt her shoulders sag. Fear was an acid in her belly that Nash would do something stupid. Gideon would be able to talk some sense into him.

Donna looked at her phone when it pinged. "He says he'll see both of you at home tonight. Six."

Freya helped Donna back to her recliner when she stumbled a bit. "We should go. You need to rest. And Brian will be here soon. You can catch him up. I'm sure he'll reach out to Gideon afterward."

Donna tossed her phone. "I hate being on the sidelines. Nash, don't make me have Brian arrest you for obstruction."

Nash headed for the door without responding to her threat.

Freya kissed her friend's brow. "Get some rest. I'll call you later."

Donna's eyes were already closing. "You better."

Chapter Ten

Nash was furious. He could feel anger tightening every muscle in his body. Not at Freya, or even Donna. He wasn't thrilled with either of them at the moment, but he was tired of this. Tired of this man getting the better of him. Since he was thirteen, this man had influenced every move he'd made in his life.

Freya caught up with him. "Nash. You're not thinking rationally."

Nash felt his temper fray. "You say that like it's a bad thing. Leave me alone, Freya."

Freya kept up. "Is this what you do? You run away?"

Nash turned on her. He caught her arm when she stumbled against him. "It beats the hell out of chasing a phantom."

Freya jumped in front of him and walked backward as he tried to get her out of his way. "He's not a ghost."

Nash veered around a couple walking and got ahead of her. "I'm sure the dead children would agree with you."

"Nash, please. Every step is a step forward."

That made him even angrier. "Out of how many, Freya?"

She was jogging beside him. "We don't know, Nash. But that doesn't mean you stop."

Nash stopped, saw an alley, and pulled her in behind him. He pressed her against the brick wall. "That's easy for you to say. You're not the reason those boys are dead."

Her eyes softened. "Ignatius. This is not your fault."

"Catalyst. Same difference."

She punched him in the shoulder. "So what, then? If he had killed you, those other boys would still be alive? He's chasing a high, Nash. He will never stop chasing it."

"Boys my age, my height. Some of those boys could be my twin. What was it about me that set him off? What was it that he saw in me?"

Freya set her hands on his forearms that still trapped her. "Maybe that's part of it. Another piece of the puzzle. What was it about you? Was there something special about you?"

"I'm so tired, Freya. Five weeks ago I didn't know there were other victims. I can feel the weight of their lost lives on my shoulders. Nothing you or Gideon say can change what lives inside me. For a time I thought my friends would drive the demons out. For a time I thought Maggie would. All of the women since; they made no difference. He's still there."

"Now you've had me. I can't drive them out either. So you drive me away instead?"

Nash saw the tears in her eyes. Guilt assailed him. "I'm a jackass."

Freya laid her palm on his cheek. "Yes, you are. But I understand. Maybe better than any of those other women."

Nash released her. "That's what Gideon said."

"He's a smart guy. So let's go back to your house. We can wait for him. I know a video game that is a great way to unwind."

The last of Nash's anger faded. He wrapped his arm

around her waist as they headed back to his car.

That evening, Gideon found them upstairs in Nash's office playing Cantwell.

Nash handed his computer controller to Freya. "You look tired."

"Got quite the data dump from Agent Lorenzo. Seems you had quite the conversation with Agent Monaco today. I certainly didn't expect to find you two playing video games when I got here."

Nash took Freya's hand when she started to rise to leave. "Freya talked me down. She's almost as good as you are."

Gideon smiled. "Yeah, but she's better looking."

Freya gave him a dirty look. "That's incredibly sexist."

Nash kissed her fingers. "Nothing but the simple truth. He's an ugly son. He says the same thing about Penny."

Gideon dropped onto the couch. "Anyway, the agent sent several files. The private school connection is a new one."

Nash got impatient when Gideon didn't say more. "So what does that mean?"

Gideon slowly nodded. "I think it means he's stalking these boys. Over the past twenty-seven years, he's only had thirteen victims. It begs the question, what is he doing the rest of the time?"

Freya grabbed her tablet. "He's watching. I'm going to start cross-referencing everyone who's worked at those schools."

Gideon yawned and stretched. "It's a good place to start. I mean, given the time in between and the different cities, it's hard to say where he's encountering these kids, but the schools make the most sense as the starting point. At least in the beginning."

Nash shut off the television. "So how do we get him to shift his focus back to me?"

Gideon's tone was dark. "I think he already has. He attacked the FBI agent working on your case. He taunted the forensic analyst who found and ran the DNA on a public street."

Nash kicked Gideon's boot. "What are you not saying?"

Gideon pulled out his phone. "His kingdom will fall."

"What?" Nash took the phone. An unknown number was listed at the top of the text message.

Gideon slid the phone from Nash's limp fingers. "He knows I'm the detective on the case here in D.C., and he wanted me to know it."

Freya pulled out her phone. "Did you have the lab trace it?"

"Burner."

Freya tossed her phone down. "Nothing can be easy."

Gideon shrugged. "It's his way of implying you without using your name."

Nash rose. "Prince Nash."

Gideon continued. "It's a very specific taunt. Not generic. I think you know him."

Freya shot Gideon an angry look. "You can't know that."

Gideon ignored her. "Only close friends and family would know we call you 'Prince.'"

Nash wanted to kiss Freya for coming to his defense. "Gideon's right. And it's what Donna alluded to. Grandfather's murder was personal. He didn't have to die.

So even if the kingdom refers to Camhion, or my grandfather, my father, or me, it amounts to the same thing. We know this guy."

Gideon nodded. "Or he knows you. I'm going to head home since I don't have to talk you off a ledge. I'm exhausted. And I'd like to see my wife. Take precautions. Be alert. This guy had a partner once; he could again. And Freya, the same goes for you. If he's watching Nash, then he's seen you and Nash together. And let's just say, you two don't give off a 'just friends' vibe."

Freya rose. "I should get home. I have to work in the morning."

Nash walked her out after Gideon left. "I'm sorry for earlier."

Freya stood on her toes and kissed him. "I get it. You can call me tonight."

Nash kissed her back. "I look forward to it."

* * *

Freya was cursing the next afternoon. Her grandpa had taught her plenty of Norwegian curse words to fill a book.

"That's a new one."

Freya waved Gideon into her office. "Not one hit on the cross-reference of school employees in the past few years. I can't go back twenty-seven years. None of that is digitized. Nothing ties these boys together, nothing other than our theory that they look like Nash. None of the same doctors, dentists, therapists, coaches. Nothing."

Gideon took a seat. "Let's go back to the beginning. We

need to look again at Cormac's associates. Then Eldridge's. Nash was too young. But all the men in their lives back in those days should be on the list."

Freya tapped a few keys. "We have the original detective's notes. He interviewed a lot of people. Each one was eventually ruled out."

"Let's just say I'm not feeling confident in the original detective. I want to talk to him too."

Freya took a moment at her computer. Gideon's phone dinged. "His address. He's very much alive and still lives in D.C."

Gideon pulled it up. "Want to go for a ride?"

Freya jumped and grabbed her MPD jacket. "Very much. I'd like to know how a thirteen-year-old boy's evidence happens to go missing in what was a high-profile case."

They were quiet on the drive. Both of them were deep in their own thoughts. The detective's address landed them in a middle-class neighborhood that was clearly on the decline.

The retired detective was less than impressive, as far as Freya was concerned. His belly hung over his sweatpants, and he had a mostly empty beer bottle in his hand. The t-shirt he wore to cover his bulk was covered in food stains.

Gideon was ever the professional. "Detective Elliot Dashevsky?"

The man had to look up considerably to meet Gideon's gaze. "I don't know why you're dragging this back into my life. I'm retired."

Gideon pushed. "May we come in? We'll try not to take up too much of your time."

The detective gave Freya a once over. "Not a cop."

Freya followed him inside. The interior smelled like cigarettes and mold. "Forensic analyst."

Gideon stayed standing but cleared a spot for Freya to take a seat. "Your list of potential perps was quite long. There were a lot of names to cover. I'm hoping you can give me your impressions: who stood out, who had motive?"

"At first, I figured it was Eldridge Camhion. His old man was standing in his way to a fortune. He also had quite a large life insurance policy on his wife and children. He had several million reasons to kill his father and his son."

Gideon gave nothing of his feelings away. "You said at first."

The man's shoulders drooped. "Alibi came through. Not that he couldn't have had a hit ordered. My superior didn't think he was good for it. So we moved on. All of Cormac Camhion's friends were the same. Old, white, and rich. All of Eldridge's friends were less old, white, and rich. Could have been blackmail. Could have been jealousy. Nothing stood out. The family was a small one. There was a sister and brother-in-law mixed in there somewhere."

"Hayden Brooks."

The older man coughed until he was wheezing. "Big scandal came out later on that one. But no motive. He was not in line to gain anything from Cormac's death or the grandson's."

Gideon took out a notebook. "What about the DNA from Nash Camhion's kidnapper?"

The man sat back. "How do you know about that? It never made it from the hospital to the lab. It was a huge screwup. The captain was furious. Here we had this huge case, and some tech lost the evidence."

Gideon snapped his fingers to get his attention back. "There was nothing in the case files about lost evidence."

The man looked at Gideon like he was crazy. "Why would it? I wasn't about to put a procedural screw-up in the case files. An administrative reprimand would have been opened. Poor bastard probably lost his job over it."

Freya leaned forward. "What was the name of the person who lost it?"

The man sneered. "Why would I care about the name of some lab tech?"

Freya straightened. "Why indeed."

"Doesn't matter much anyway. The case went cold fast. No one cared if it got solved or not. It was all about politics. The mayor was getting ready to announce the new Police Chief. The mayor was also up for reelection that year. Ended up winning, too. The old chief was blamed for the lack of evidence and leads in the case. The mayor made sure to throw him under the bus to make himself look good. The chief was only chief for a few more months before he was killed, and a new one was appointed. He was days away from being officially fired when he was killed in a hit-and-run."

Gideon jotted it all down. "The case file is thin on Nash Camhion's kidnapping."

The man shrugged. "Like I said, it was an election year. The murder of Cormac Camhion was huge news, and I was given explicit instructions that the kidnapping had better not make the evening news. Besides, the person who killed the old man was the same man who kidnapped Nash

Camhion.   So what did it matter which case was investigated?"

Gideon's hand fisted.   "It mattered.   What about the second man who grabbed Nash and drove the van?"

"Kid only recalled one perpetrator during his so-called captivity. Guy was probably paid to snatch the kid and then disappeared. There were no fingerprints, no leads on the second man.   Personally, I wondered if there was a kidnapping at all. The whole thing could have been staged. Eyewitness accounts were that Nash Camhion was dragged from the scene by a good Samaritan. Kid wasn't talking. No one came forward."

Gideon swore. "That's the line that was fed the press. We both know it's a pile of crap. You saw where Nash had been held. His injuries were fully documented. He clearly was a victim."

The detective shrugged.   "It was a long time ago. Memory isn't what it used to be."

There wasn't much more the detective had to share, and then he outright refused to answer any more questions.

Gideon swore and headed for the door. Freya followed him out.

"Guy would lie about his own mother to save his hide." Freya zipped her jacket.

Gideon unlocked the car. "Nash's dad was campaigning that year to be the next mayor. We should talk to Nash."

Freya agreed.   "Maybe he remembers a few of the players. I noticed you didn't tell him you were the kid who saved Nash."

Gideon started the engine. "No point. Like you said,

he'd lie about his own mother. And a different detective had interviewed me. Detectives like him give cops a bad name."

Freya felt the same. "I'm assuming you went back over all the names in the files yourself. You wouldn't have trusted the detective's original assessments."

"No, I didn't. I ran them. But for a long time, I investigated this under the Camhion's radar. Penny didn't even know I was investigating it until she came across the file in my apartment. I never questioned Eldridge directly."

Freya sighed. "It's inevitable at this point."

Gideon gripped the steering wheel hard enough for it to creak. "We'll start with Nash. But Eldridge is next."

They found Nash at his computer. His eyes were glued to the screen. Gideon closed the door behind them. "Hey."

Nash tapped a few keys and looked up. His eyes went to Freya. "Hi."

Gideon couldn't help the smile. "You got it bad."

Nash's brow rose but didn't argue. "Why do I have the pleasure of both of you here?"

Gideon took a seat. Freya came and stood beside Gideon. She was the one that spoke. They both thought it might be easier if she asked. "We had some questions about your dad's mayoral campaign."

Nash leaned back in his seat. His eyes held hers. "Not sure what there is to know. My dad was going to run for mayor. Never did. When I was a kid, he campaigned and tried to gather backers for a couple of years. That's how I met Isaac. My dad had invited a bunch of businessmen, professors, and politicians over for a party. Isaac's dad was there. So were dozens of other people."

Freya took a seat. "Gideon and I met with the detective who investigated your and your grandfather's case."

Nash's laugh was harsh. "Ah, yes. Detective Elliot Dashevsky. He was in charge. I remember him well. He came by the house a few times. I would sit at the top of the stairs while my father grilled him on the progress, or lack thereof, on Grandfather's case. My dad feared someone might try to grab me again. And he feared for Penny. Even in Baltimore, my dad had guards watching her and Grandmother. None of us went alone anywhere for years. The detective was not sympathetic. In crude words, he told my dad he could afford around-the-clock protection, so he could deal with it. I don't recall the detective coming by again after a couple of months. No doubt my dad filed a complaint, but it didn't matter. There were no more leads."

Nash pushed back from his desk. "When I got a little older, I sought the man out. Within five minutes I knew he wasn't working on the case and hadn't for years. He flat-out refused to talk to me. Said he'd passed it off as a cold case and wasn't going to waste another moment on it."

Freya folded her hands on her lap. "According to the detective, he is aware that your evidence was lost. He said a tech lost it. He didn't document its loss."

Nash considered that. "So what do you think happened?"

Gideon rubbed his tired eyes. "I don't know. It could simply be that the tech lost it. It could be that it got mixed up with your grandfather's evidence. It could be that someone purposefully hid it, and when the case went cold, decided to store it away. Or maybe someone wanted it to be found and placed it there for someone to find."

Freya dropped her head. "Too many questions and not enough answers."

Nash scooted forward in his chair. "Come on, now. That's my line. I need you to be the optimistic one. Gideon and I are too jaded."

Freya gave him a small smile. "My apologies. I want to find out who the tech was. Detective Dashevsky didn't know."

Gideon laughed. "He hit a hot button. You should have seen the look Freya gave him. Had he actually been looking at her, he might have had a heart attack right there."

"I hate detectives who don't take the work that forensic analysts do seriously."

Nash took her hand and kissed her knuckles. "I do."

Gideon interrupted. "None of that. We need to focus. I want to talk to your dad."

Nash let her hand go. "I'd like to keep my mom out of it."

"I can do that. I'll have Penny set up time at Camhion. It won't look odd for him to pop in to visit."

Nash leaned back in his chair. "What about the schools and the knife?"

Freya's sigh blew her bangs away from her face. "No crossovers that I can find. At least not in the past few years. Without going to each school and getting the old employment records, I'm stymied. The knife is faring a little better. I've emailed the composite we made, and I've found a few people who custom-make similar knives.

Unfortunately, our guy could have bought it anywhere in the country. We know he likes to travel. But since this started in D.C., that's where I'm starting. And using photographs, we're as sure as we can be that he's used the same knife on each victim. I've got some names, but other vendors want a warrant. I'm going to start with the stacks of receipts I do have. But with the FBI saying Donna's attack was not related to the Henney case, no warrant. Not today."

Nash's frustration was back. "Everywhere we turn we're blocked. We can't get a warrant. We can't get school records. We can't know where the knife came from. We don't know who the analyst was that took the sample. We don't know who the partner was."

Gideon interrupted. "Puzzle pieces, Nash. Eventually they'll connect."

Nash's jaw clenched. "I hope you're right."

Chapter Eleven

Eldridge thought back to thirty years ago. "Affordable housing. That was the main reason I decided I wanted to run for mayor. There is so much money circulating in D.C., and yet folks struggle to find affordable places to live. Dad's first venture was building new apartment buildings. I built on that, expanding into storefronts and other rental buildings. But housing has always been a passion. And a problem we still have to this day."

Freya flipped through the list of names Eldridge had provided of the donors he could remember. "There are some big names on this list."

He nodded. "Ansel Reddick was by far the biggest. He still invests in some of the building projects Penny spearheads. He also builds quite a few of his own. But he develops and sells. He's not a fan of people. Greg Chalmers. Now he was probably the second biggest. He had ties with the city's public works department. He always thought more could be done to improve the city. Isaac's dad. He contributed some funds while sticking his nose up in the air. But he liked to pretend he cared, and he thought aligning with me, and in turn Camhion Enterprises, might be worthwhile. I knew the Chief of Police back then, too. I liked the man, and he had a lot of ideas on how to combat crime."

Freya set the list down. "Why didn't you run?"

Eldridge rubbed the tension in his brow. "Nash. I never knew if putting myself in the public eye had something to do with his abduction. In some ways, I could understand coming after my dad. He was not a quiet man, and if he had an opinion, he was going to share it. But to come after my son; I never could wrap my mind around it."

Gideon stepped forward. "Money. It's often that simple. You had something the kidnapper didn't. Or wanted more of. That ransom you paid was hefty."

Nash disagreed. It was more. So much more. "Money seemed the motive because it was the obvious one. This guy didn't care about money. Unless it was a way to secure a place to torture and kill. It was the thrill of it. The excitement. Even the control. I realize he made off with a fortune, but even if you had refused to pay, he got what he wanted."

Freya agreed. "For men like him, money would be inconsequential. But he's also smart. Had he not asked for ransom, that would have raised even more questions. Kill Cormac, take Nash, get the money, and kill the victim. All neat and tidy. But this wasn't as neat and tidy as it appeared. Do you remember anyone else besides Detective Dashevsky?"

"Nurses and doctors. One particular doctor, Dr. Seth Barry. He was able to calm Nash down and was the one who got him talking again. Had a way with kids. Nurses came and went. I don't remember. And police, well, there were too many to count. The detective was the one I worked with the most. Because I knew the Chief, he stayed out of it. It was in his best interests, and he didn't want there to be any hint of favoritism or conflict of interest."

Freya jotted down a few more notes. "Do you remember anyone else? The DNA that went missing was collected by a tech, but no one seems to remember him."

"Like the nurses, people from the police department came and went. No one was memorable."

Nash felt her frustration. "There really were too many people. I remember wanting to scream for everyone to get out. But during the medical exam, I had been given some anxiety medication, and most of it was a blur."

Freya tucked the tablet in her purse. "I need my computer. I need to find the tech."

Gideon agreed. "We need to try again to find that money. The ransom had to be deposited somewhere."

Nash walked the two of them to the elevator door. "I'll hitch a ride with Dad. Pick you up tonight?"

Freya leaned in for a kiss. "I should be home by seven. Henry will be out tonight. Poker game. If you promise to drive me to work tomorrow, I'll pack an overnight bag."

The others in the room pretended not to notice when he kissed Freya. The very public display was not like him, but Nash needed to touch her. "Seven."

Freya and Gideon headed for the elevator, and Nash followed his dad outside after they stopped in to see Penny.

"You two seem serious." Ten minutes later, Eldridge was headed toward Nash's home.

Nash watched the scenery but wasn't really seeing it. "Too serious. It's like a moth to a flame. I know I should keep away, but everything inside me draws me back to her.

I keep thinking how I didn't want to meet her. I wanted her to be a fantasy on the other side of the phone. But since the moment I saw her, I wanted her. I have this desire to see her. To touch her to make sure she's real."

"Well, son, she looked pretty real to me. With the right woman, there is nothing to fear."

"She feels right." It was the only way Nash could describe what he felt. This inevitability. And it felt good.

"Your three friends are happy. They set a great example of what love should look like."

Love. That word. Freya was right. He did know what love was. And he loved her. He had no other words for what she made him feel. Lust was easy. Attraction was easy. Desire was easy. But this was more. And damned if it wasn't just as easy. At least with her.

Eldridge's words interrupted Nash's spiraling thoughts. "My dad used to talk to me about legacy. He loved his work, but it didn't define him. His family did. When you were born, he held you and cried. He had such high hopes. And when Penny was born, he kissed her brow and vowed to always protect her. He loved both of you equally. But he wanted his name and future generations to live on through you."

Nash felt emotion clogging his throat. "I know. He made it sound wonderful. That a piece of him and a piece of you would live on through me, and so on and so on. It didn't feel like a burden back then. It felt right. But Dad, what if I can't protect my children?"

Eldridge pulled off the road. "Is that what this is about? Cormac's failure? My failure?"

Nash's hands fisted. "It hurts to say it, but yes. He failed. You failed. I don't know how you survived it. And the scary part is there was nothing at all you could have done. No one saw this man coming."

Eldridge took his son's hand and undid the fist. "Maybe that's the difference, Nash. Cormac and I didn't see him coming. But you do. You know what's out there. And you know how to keep your children safe; you're prepared in ways I never was. Freya, she too knows what is out there. Between the two of you, there is no one you can't stop. And when you find this sick bastard, maybe you'll believe that."

* * *

Freya started pacing. It didn't get past her that she'd picked the habit up from Nash. "How can we not know who this guy was? How can employment records for every male who worked in the forensic lab just disappear?"

Captain Barnes sat calmly in his seat. "I don't know, Ms. Jensen. But perhaps I can help. Erroll Jackson. He still works in recruiting. He will know, or he'll know who would know."

Freya didn't wait for the captain to dismiss her. She headed across the building. Mr. Jackson was easy to find. He had his own office, stood six and a half feet tall, and his snow-white hair was a stark contrast to his dark complexion.

"Ms. Jensen. What brings you my way?"

"Records are missing."

His white brow lifted, and he took offense at her tone.

"Quite an accusation. I run this office with military precision."

Freya took a deep breath and explained what she was looking for and what had happened.

The older man confirmed what she said. "Well, now. This would be before my time at this desk. All the old files were scanned. But I'm a believer in the old ways."

She watched as he dug out a set of keys and pulled one ringed with orange plastic. "Storage room 227. It will take you forever, but all the old papers are there."

She started to bolt.

"And Ms. Jensen. You will tell me what you find."

"Yes, sir."

The storage room smelled much like she thought it would. The room had the smell of an old library. However, it was not as organized as one. It took twenty minutes to decipher the filing system, what there was of it, and another two hours to find the right boxes. Thousands of employment records were in the boxes.

In her lab, hours later, she found what she was looking for. She immediately dialed Gideon. "Get down here."

Five minutes later, Gideon was in her doorway.

Freya started shoving boxes his way. "I need your eyes. You know the names better. These are the employment records of every person who worked here during the year of Nash's kidnapping."

Gideon started thumbing through. "Performance evaluations."

"And we know the tech was male."

"How?"

Freya was quickly sorting. "Computer employment records for all the lab workers from that year were missing. Or I should say all the files on the male workers were missing. Jackson down in recruiting said we kept all the paper records after they were scanned. So they were removed from the computer, but the papers were kept."

Gideon started sorting the box she shoved his way. "I knew there was a reason I hated computers."

Freya continued. "And honestly, how often are old records accessed? There's no telling how long they've been missing."

Hours later, Freya found reprimands. "These. Maybe our guy is in here."

Gideon took the stack from her. "Freya, it's late. We're both cross-eyed and hungry. I'll lock these in my desk, and we can start fresh tomorrow. Besides, you made a date with Nash."

She shivered in anticipation. "So I did."

She bid Gideon good night, closed up her office, and made her way home. The sun was setting, and rush hour traffic had thinned. Henry was gone by the time she got home. She stripped and took a quick shower.

When she stepped out of the shower, she heard her phone. She smiled, thinking it was Nash. But it wasn't.

Stop digging, Princess. You won't live to regret it.

Freya felt dizzy and dropped the phone. Once the dizziness passed, she ran into the living room, naked and dripping water. She grabbed her laptop, and the reverse trace told her what she expected. A burner. She swore and then dialed Gideon.

"Eginhard."

"I got a text. A threat." She rattled off the message.

"Trace?"

Freya's frustration was palpable. "Burner. Same as your call. I don't like the princess bit."

The sound of rattling keys came over the line as Gideon spoke. "Not much we can do. But I don't like it either. He didn't threaten me, but he beat Agent Monaco badly enough to land her in intensive care. And this guy knows what you look like. I'm going to have a trace put on your phone. There is already one on mine."

Freya ran her hands through her hair, realizing she was still naked in the living room. Cursing, she headed back to her room for a towel. "Should I ignore it?"

"Ignore it. We can't know how he might react to a response."

Freya glanced around the bedroom. A photo of her with her grandparents caught her attention. "I can't bring this into Grandpa Henry's home."

Gideon heard her unspoken words. "Is there somewhere else you can stay? Maybe Henry can stay?"

Freya's eyes watered and the room spun a little. Swallowing hard, she laid down. "Henry is out tonight. I don't want to frighten him, but I don't want him to come home. We can't be sure this guy hasn't been following us."

The sound of Gideon's car door slamming was loud in Freya's ear. "I'm heading your way. I'll take a look around. This guy is smart, and it's highly unlikely he's been near your home. But I'd rather be certain."

Freya closed her eyes. "Nash should be here soon. I was

going to his place."

"Across the street from a cop is a great place to hide out."

"Subtle, Detective."

Gideon laughed despite the tension. "Trust me. You might as well pack a bag for an extended stay. Nash is not going to let you go home. We'll talk when I get there. For now, make sure you're locked up tight. And if you own a firearm, keep it nearby."

Freya waited until the room settled, and she slowly sat up. Her stomach was roiling, and her knees felt weak. She'd never had her life threatened before. Apparently, it didn't agree with her. Taking calming breaths, she pulled her robe on before checking all the locks. She did own a firearm. She'd learned how to shoot and got a license not long after she started studying forensics. She knew firsthand what people were capable of doing to each other. She hadn't initially gone into law enforcement, but she had great respect for the work they did.

She took the firearm out of a box on her bookcase and took off the gun lock. She set it on her dresser while she pulled on a pair of worn jeans and a slouchy sweater. She grabbed her suitcase and tossed it on her bed. The suitcase was an old, battered piece, but she was fond of it. It had belonged to her parents.

Freya stopped after she opened her closet door and stared at its contents. What was she doing? She couldn't stay with Nash, could she? Going from having sex to moving in was a big leap, even under the circumstances. She should call Donna. She should pack her bag and go to her apartment. But with Donna off the case, wasn't she safe? If she went there, would she bring him back into Donna's life?

Heart pounding and mind racing, she packed. Work clothes, underwear, her nightgown. What else? She tossed the toiletries from her bathroom into the suitcase. In a desperate need to feel some control, she put the picture of her and her grandparents on top.

She zipped it up and sat in her bedroom. Fifteen minutes later, there was a knock on her front door, and she heard Gideon's voice. She set the gun down on the side table and opened the door.

"Perimeter is clear. There is no sign of anyone on your property."

She closed and locked the door behind him. "So now what?"

Gideon picked up her pistol, looked it over, and checked the clip. "You know how to use this?"

"Yes. And I have a license for it."

Gideon set it down. "Not a bad idea to pack it. Did you call Nash?"

She heard another car pull into the driveway. "No. And I'm betting that's him."

Gideon pulled the curtain and saw Nash. He unlocked the door. "Come on in."

Nash gave Freya a once over. "Everything okay?"

Gideon gestured to the living room. "We should sit."

Nash was on full alert. "What happened?"

Freya's knees wobbled. "You might not want to sit, but I do."

Nash threw Gideon a look that demanded he start

talking as he led Freya to the sofa.

Gideon sat across from them. "Freya got a text. Similar to mine. Except he threatened her."

Nash's hands balled at his sides. "What kind of threat?"

Freya handed Nash her phone. "The 'leave it alone or you'll regret it' kind."

Nash stared at the message. "Why isn't he coming at me?"

Gideon set his hand over Nash's. "The better question is how does he know so much about the investigation? He knew about Agent Monaco. He got my phone number. Now Freya. He knows about your relationship with her."

Nash's hand trembled. "He called her Princess."

"To your prince. I don't like this new game he's playing. But the more he reveals himself, the more likely he is to make a mistake."

Nash's eyes hardened. He turned to Freya. "Pack a bag."

Gideon smiled at Freya. "I already told her to."

Nash took Freya's hand. "Let's go get your things. Did you call Henry?"

Freya took a deep breath, trying to get herself under control. "No. I was hoping maybe Gideon, you could call him? If I call him, he'll want to come rushing over here. Maybe you can keep him calm enough not to come charging in. I don't want him hurt."

Gideon set a hand on her shoulder. "I will. I've talked a few people off the ledge over the years. Just promise me you'll stay with Nash. I'll drive you to work tomorrow. And we'll go back to the files."

Freya nodded, and Nash followed her to her bedroom. "I

think I've got everything."

Nash glanced around her room. "You're not a high-maintenance kind of female."

She glanced around. The room was neat and tidy, the paint a light blue, her bedding a deep purple. Other than a dresser and a bookcase stuffed with books and a few trinkets, the room was pretty bare. "I guess not. Is that good or bad?"

Nash pulled her to him. She wrapped her arms around him and absorbed some of his strength. He brushed the hair from her temples. "Neither I suppose. Just an observation."

She pulled away. She glanced around the room. She then grabbed her locket from her jewelry box. She tucked it carefully into the lining of her suitcase. "I could go to Donna's."

Nash stopped as he went to grab her suitcase. "Is that where you want to go?"

She couldn't read the look on his face. She opted for the truth. "No."

Nash cupped her face and lightly kissed her. "Let's go."

Gideon was waiting for them in the living room. She took the gun lock she'd grabbed off her dresser. She locked the gun and tucked it into her suitcase. She felt Nash's eyes on her, but she didn't dare look at him.

Gideon walked them out. "I'll pick you up at eight. Try to get some rest."

Nash set her suitcase in the trunk and came around to hold the door. "Come on. I'd like to get out of the open."

She was tense on the drive to Nash's. What she had hoped would be another night like the last time was dashed.

Nash didn't say anything to her on the way to his house. She honestly didn't know what to say either.

But his words, once they were locked inside his house, weren't the ones she expected to hear.

Nash set her suitcase down. "I'm so sorry, Freya. I never imagined he would come after you."

His apology and the serious look on his face upset her. "I'm not feeling well."

Taking her hand and her suitcase, he led her to his bedroom. "Why don't you lie down, and I'll clear some room for your things."

Unable to argue, she lay down on her side and pulled her knees to her chest. Her stomach hurt and her head was pounding. She watched as he pushed some of his clothes over to make room for hers. She didn't argue when he emptied her suitcase. He cleared a drawer out and tossed the rest of her things in it.

Nash came back to her after putting her toiletries in his bathroom. He put a hand on her brow. "How do you feel?"

She took his hand. She felt overwhelmingly tired. "Please don't be sorry, Ignatius. No matter who he is, we'll find him. And we'll end this."

"I know we will."

His lips on hers were the last thing she felt before drifting off to sleep.

* * *

Nash laid down and held her while she slept. She was exhausted. Her skin was practically translucent, and the bruises under her eyes were darker than he'd ever seen them. Guilt gnawed at him. He'd brought a killer into her world. He had nothing good to bring into her life. Now she was being threatened, and it was his fault. He should have stayed away. He should have been able to control himself around her. He should have stuck to his gut reaction to let this go.

But pictures of dead boys haunted his dreams. Boys whose deaths he felt weighing on his shoulders. He needed to be strong. For her. For them.

Nash's phone buzzed. Gideon assured him Henry was safe and was going to stay with a friend. An officer would escort him tomorrow to pack a few things. He sent his thanks. His phone buzzed again. Trenton sent a note to reach out if he needed anything. Isaac was last and said the same thing. He felt the love of his friends surrounding him. He felt a sudden fierce love and need to protect Freya. He stripped off her shoes and pulled the blankets over them. She was safe tonight. And he vowed he'd do anything to keep her that way.

Chapter Twelve

Freya woke to callused hands stroking the skin of her belly. Nash's warm breath was on her neck. Faint morning sunlight was peeking through the blinds. She felt his fingers undoing the buttons of her slacks. Desire pooled in her belly as his fingers danced over her skin.

Nash kissed the back of her neck. He slid his hands so that he could pull her shirt over her head. Clever fingers slipped under her sports bra and stroked her breasts. She felt them swell under his ministrations. Laying with her back to him, he finished undressing her. She felt his erection pressing between her thighs, but he didn't seem to be in a hurry. His entire body stroked hers from behind, and she'd never felt anything half as erotic. Her eyes were still closed, her body arching into his. He draped one of her thighs over his and she felt him move into her. Just ever so slightly.

He kissed the back of her neck and tormented her with his fingers. She tried to bring him further inside her, but he held her hips still. He seemed content to tease her. He didn't say a word to her. Eventually he shifted to his knees and brought her up with him, her back pressed to his chest. She heard the soft whimpers coming from the back of her throat, but he didn't heed them. He stayed partially inside her, his hands on her breasts, his teeth and lips on her neck.

She found herself leaning forward, her hands on his headboard. He rose up behind her and pulled her onto him. She felt tears sting her eyes at the fullness of him. She could feel him deep inside. He held her hips still, one arm around her waist, one hand on top of hers.

He whispered in her ear. "Mine."

One shift of his hips and she convulsed around him. Her vision grayed and she could barely breathe at the intensity of it. She felt him follow her as his hips ground against her. She would have collapsed but he held her to him. He held her for a time before releasing her and she slid onto the bed. He rested beside her, his fingers wiping the tears from her cheeks. His gray eyes held hers.

Nash continued to stroke her cheek as she got herself under control.

When the tears dried up, Nash shifted and pulled her against his chest. "It wasn't supposed to be like this."

Freya wrapped herself around him, one thigh resting between his. "Like what?"

Nash hugged her tighter. "I wasn't supposed to fall in love with you. I wasn't supposed to want all the things I told myself I didn't need."

Freya propped her hands on his chest so she could see his face. "You're serious."

Nash's eyes held hers again. "I didn't want to get married. Not even to Maggie. I didn't want to have children. I know what lies in the shadows. I didn't want to lose any more than I already had. But more than those things, I don't want to lose you. I don't have soft words for you, Freya. I don't know what the future holds. I just know that I need you in mine."

Freya rose and straddled him. She used her hands to push him onto his back. "I loved you before I even met you. The only thing that would make me leave you is you."

Nash sat up again, so they were pressed together, chest to breast. "Not even then, if I recall."

All the residual tension and fear she had felt yesterday drained from her. "You didn't mean it."

Nash kissed her. "No. I didn't."

Freya lingered over the kiss. "I need to wash up."

Nash lifted her, set her on her feet, took her hand, and led her to the shower. "Gideon will be here soon."

They took a quick shower, though their hands lingered on each other as they washed. She was drying off when he came up behind her again. "Are you okay?"

She nodded. "Never showered with a man before."

Nash hid his smile behind her shoulder. "Your education is sorely lacking."

Freya leaned into him. "You're a great teacher."

Nash followed her into the bedroom. He frowned as he looked at the bed. "Are you on the pill, Freya?"

She stopped in her tracks. "No."

Nash swore.

Freya suddenly felt cold. She quickly grabbed her clothes and got dressed.

Nash stood in the doorway of the bedroom so she couldn't leave. "I'm sorry. I meant it. I don't want children."

Freya tried to get past him. "Don't worry about it. It's my problem."

Nash crowded her back into the bedroom. "It is not your problem. It's our problem. I wasn't thinking."

Freya didn't bother to tell him, not for the first time. She didn't think he realized they'd had unprotected sex that first time. "As Grandpa Henry would say, don't borrow trouble."

Nash took a deep breath. "Smart man. You'll tell me."

She dropped her gaze. "Sure."

Freya left the bedroom and went to the kitchen. "I need coffee."

Nash went about making it. "You need to eat."

Freya didn't think she could. "Having a crazy man threaten to kill me ruined my appetite. Just coffee."

Nash was going to say something when there was a knock at the door. "Gideon."

Freya took the cup Nash handed her. She watched as Gideon came into the room. She had no doubt he could feel the tension between them. She took a few swallows before setting it aside. "Let me brush my teeth and grab my things."

Freya could hear their voices as she fled to the bathroom. She heard Gideon ask what Nash had done now. She blocked out the ensuing argument.

Taking a deep breath, she grabbed her things. She had a case to solve.

* * *

Nash fretted most of the day. He couldn't seem to keep his mouth shut. One minute he told Freya he loved her, and the next he basically told her he didn't want to commit to her. When he stared at the bed, he realized he hadn't used the condoms in the drawer. He'd broken out in a cold sweat. But she'd made him mad when she said it was her problem. As if he wasn't part of the equation.

Knowing he needed a clear head, and since it was summer, he went to find Isaac. He knew Isaac was at home working on his latest novel. Lilah was working from home, taking time off from Cantwell to work on the art for the second graphic novel she and Isaac were writing. It had been a brilliant idea, if he said so himself, to suggest to Isaac that he write the novels. And to push Lilah his way. Nash, the man who didn't want to get married and have kids, wasn't a bad matchmaker. He'd had to shove Gideon to make a move on Penny. Trenton, well, Trenton knew what he wanted and went after it. Isaac would have kept plodding along had Nash not shoved.

Isaac opened the door. "You look terrible."

Nash slapped his friend on the shoulder. "I can always trust you to tell me like it is."

Isaac gestured to him to head to the kitchen. "It's what I'm for. I'm making lunch. Lilah is grumbling at me, so I'm trying to butter her up with lunch."

Nash took a seat at the island. Isaac was an amazing chef. If his books ever stopped selling, he could open his own restaurant. "I could use some buttering up, too."

"No doubt. How is the investigation coming?"

Nash's shoulders straightened. "He threatened Freya."

Isaac turned. His usual calm demeanor changed. "Gideon told me the guy texted him. When did he threaten Freya?"

Nash glanced at his fists. "Last night. She's staying with me for now. She hitched a ride to work with Gideon, so she's safe at work. I need a level head."

Isaac set about fixing lunch. "I'm your man. What do you need leveling?"

"I might have gotten Freya pregnant."

Isaac stopped. "When?"

Nash waved his hand. "This morning."

Isaac took a seat, lunch forgotten. "And you don't want children. What did you say?"

Nash grunted. "The wrong thing. What else?"

Isaac set his hands on the counter. "I want children. It's funny because my dad was an awful parent. My mom was emotionally absent. And yet, deep down, I knew that's not how things were supposed to be. I like to think I would do better. You went through a trauma. But you know that's not how things are supposed to be. And you know deep down that the chances of something like that happening to your children are zero. Tell me, if she's pregnant, what do you do? You push her away? Tell her to get rid of it?"

Fury settled in his belly. "Never."

Isaac went back to lunch. "You'd do whatever you had to do to protect her and the child. So what are you worried about?"

Nash opened his mouth, but no words came out. He leaned back in his seat. "That's what I love about you. No mincing of words."

Lilah peeked around the corner. "It's also one of his flaws. But I love him anyway. I thought I heard voices. I can go away."

Nash waved her in. "Just man talk. We're done."

Lilah took a seat next to him. "Women trouble?"

Isaac leaned in to kiss her. "The best kind to have."

She murmured against his mouth. "You have to say that. I'm annoyed with you."

Isaac didn't disagree. He went back to fixing lunch.

Nash's phone buzzed. "Trenton."

Isaac set lunch down. "Is he next on your list?"

"Yeah. Figured he'd be good for some advice."

Lilah stopped mid-bite. "What is going on?"

Nash kissed her cheek. "I'm in love with Freya."

"Oh. That's nice. I didn't think you'd ever fall in love."

He shrugged. "Me, neither."

Lilah bent her head so she could look up at Nash. "Are you okay?"

Nash assured her he was. "It's funny, I asked Freya the same question. But I'm fine. She's fine. Just working out the kinks in our relationship."

Lilah looked skeptical, but she remained silent as they ate.

An hour later, Isaac walked him to the door. "Good luck with Trenton. I'll text him to be on his best behavior."

Nash appreciated it. But he had nothing to worry about. Trenton was serious when he opened the door.

"I hear you're in love with Freya."

Nash looked around for Trenton's family. "Are you here by yourself?"

"Ginny is at work. Gwenny is having a play date. We're good to talk. Though I do hear I'm last on the list."

Nash followed Trenton inside. "I was saving the best for

last."

"Nice save, Prince Nash. Not sure I can help. Isaac usually is the best at these types of things."

"You're a parent. None of us are."

Trenton handed Nash a beer. "Scary thing, being a parent. Especially when you don't start at the beginning."

Gwenny was Trenton's step-daughter. He was also the only father Gwenny ever had. "Do you think about having kids?"

"Sure. Penny and Gideon are trying. I figure Lilah and Isaac won't be far behind. And none of us are getting any younger. So, yes, I want to have kids. Growing up in a cult, I never thought I'd have a normal relationship. But Ginny understands me. She grew up the way I did, so we have that common ground. She told me once she didn't want to have kids. But it was more the circumstances. She wasn't going to have a child raised in a cult. So we talk about it. Gwenny is settled in. And it's time."

Nash adored Gwenny. She was full of sass and unconditional love. "You and I never thought we would get married and have kids."

Trenton took a pull on his beer. "You were adamant that you would never get married. I just figured it wouldn't happen. There's a difference."

"So what's your advice?"

"Get to it already. You'll be a great dad. And your kids will have amazing grandparents. And an amazing aunt. And you're not alone, Nash. You've got three best friends and a family who love and support you. And if Freya is willing to put up with you and your moods, then I'd say you're a lucky man indeed."

* * *

Across town, Freya wasn't feeling lucky. She was frustrated. She'd narrowed her choices down to three techs. The first was not their guy. He was serving time for fraud and doctoring records. He would have been in prison when the last child was murdered. The second was not better. He was still working but in Arizona. She had lots of electronic trails that showed he was there right now. Seemed unlikely.

The third man was the most promising. Warren Stanich had a handful of reprimands on file from almost thirty years ago. Eventually the man had quit. He'd gotten into teaching seminars to people who thought solving crimes was like television. He was selling them a dream, and that ticked her off. Today he was living right here in D.C. He was barely able to pay his rent on an apartment he lived in. If he owned a home where he could keep kids undetected, she couldn't find one. And there was nothing in this guy's history to suggest he was a killer. But right now, he was at the top of the list.

Gideon came in not an hour later. "Check your inbox."

Freya pulled up the interoffice email. She swore. "How did you find this?"

"Theory is Nash knows this guy. We also figure this has something to do with either Cormac or Eldridge. Our friend Detective Dashevsky didn't even investigate half these guys. Judge signed off on a warrant to do a check of old bank records. And I got a hit."

"Ansel Reddick. He's a friend of Nash's dad, isn't he?"

"Bastard is one of the top investors and on the board of Camhion. Guy was at my wedding."

Freya's stomach clenched. "Two million. Is that what a boy's life is worth?"

Gideon put a hand on her to steady her. "You're pale. Did you eat?"

Freya shook her head. "Coffee. Not hungry."

"Let's get some food in you. I need you to dig into this guy."

A bowl of soup and crackers, and an hour later, Freya was nose-deep in her laptop. "He's got a lot of money. This guy didn't need the ransom, I can tell you that. He's the father of two. One divorce. Messy. Oldest son works for him. Younger son, too. He's a lawyer. Same class as Nash when Nash was abducted."

"He and Nash are not friends. Nash can't stand him. But it's also not surprising they were in the same school. Lots of money and prestige inside those school walls."

Freya hummed. "I also dug into Hayden Brooks like you asked. That guy is shady. Lots of odd expenses. Way more going out than he has coming in. Camhion Enterprises pays him well. And you said he is sick. I can safely say he's not faking it. Phone records have him calling several different doctors. A few lawyers, too."

Gideon checked his gun. "I need to talk to Ansel. Want to come? I could use a second set of eyes."

Freya grabbed her jacket. "I'd love to."

They weren't even ten minutes into the interview when Freya decided Ansel Reddick had no idea what they were talking about. Freya sat quietly off to the side and watched.

Gideon set the paper in front of him. "There is no mistake. The exact sum of what Eldridge Camhion wired to Nash's kidnappers was found in your bank account within days. If Detective Dashevsky had bothered to check, you would have had this conversation twenty-seven years ago. And likely you'd be in prison for murder and kidnapping."

The man paled. "I didn't do this. I have no idea how this got into my account. I wasn't involved. Eldridge is a friend. I never would have done something like this."

Gideon continued to rattle off dates. Not surprisingly, the man claimed he couldn't remember where he was during the times the other boys were murdered. But the last one struck a nerve.

"Where were you?"

Ansel stammered. "I was here in D.C. The project I was working on was wrapping up. It's the same building I'm trying to convince Penelope Camhion to purchase. I would have been within miles of the building. I think I need a lawyer."

Gideon took a step back. "It's certainly your right. I'll be getting a warrant to check all of your accounts. The next time I see you, it will be to take you downtown. Keep that lawyer handy."

Freya followed Gideon out. "He had no idea what you were talking about. Not a twitch. It wasn't until the last murder that he showed any emotion."

Gideon ran a hand through his hair, his frustration palpable. "It's not him. He could be the second man, but he's not our murderer. One, he's too old. Nash's kidnapper was younger. Second, even if he looked young, he has the wrong color eyes."

Freya shared his frustration. "Suppose it was too much to hope it would be that easy. But the money was there. I don't like coincidences."

"Same. So let's find some overlap between Eldridge and Ansel. Let's see who might be tied to our possible tech. And let's go talk to that tech."

Two hours later, Warren Stanich was stammering and trying to avoid answering direct questions. It didn't take a cop's intuition to know that the forensic tech was lying through his teeth. This time, Gideon sat to the side.

Freya spun the paper. "That's a DNA result from the kit you took at the hospital. That DNA is tied to several murders and is currently under investigation by the FBI. Your name and your file are already on their desk."

The man was in his late fifties. He kept his blond hair short and slicked back with too much hair gel. The suit he wore was tailored to fit his thin frame. He looked like the snake oil salesman he was. He was sweating profusely, his eyes kept darting away, and he knew exactly what she was talking about.

"This is the reprimand with your name on it. Seems you lost quite a few samples in your short time at the lab. You lasted, what, another year before you were fired?"

"I wasn't fired; I quit. The whole thing was a set up. My boss didn't like me. He must have stolen the samples to get me in trouble."

The idea was ludicrous, so she thwarted it. "You had two different bosses. Both were after you?"

He wiped the sweat from his brow. "Well, yes. I admit I took the swab. But I didn't lose the evidence. Things get lost in storage all the time. Too much evidence."

Freya smiled. "I didn't say it was lost in storage. I said it was lost."

Gideon stepped in. "You'll need to come downtown."

* * *

Nash sat in a conference room watching the video of Gideon's interrogation. The sound was off, so he could see the man but not hear. He stood next to Freya, who had walked him over to watch the video. "He's not the man who kidnapped me. At least, I don't think it's him."

Freya kept her distance. "It was a long time ago. You said you didn't get a good look at him. But Gideon doesn't recognize him either. And he said Ansel Reddick was too old and had the wrong eye color."

"The second man. He was white. Blond. I was so focused on my grandfather that's all I remember about the second man. He could have been anyone. Even this guy. In my mind, he was a lot bigger."

Freya struggled to keep her distance and stay objective, but couldn't keep away. She took his hand in hers. "A child's perception. Gideon, too. And it was so long ago. Eyewitnesses are notoriously wrong. Even Gideon's recollection can't be completely trusted."

Nash's jaw was clenched as he continued to stare at the man on the video. "So now what?"

Freya glanced at the clock. "Now I put in overtime.

Gideon puts the pressure on, and I dig. You should go home."

Nash squeezed her hand. "I suppose. Walk me out?"

Freya kept her hand in his as they walked outside. She stood by his car. "I'll keep you posted."

Nash took her in his arms. "Make sure Gideon drives you home. Or I can come get you."

Freya leaned into him. "Gideon will be at it all night. I'll call you."

He kissed her before releasing her. Neither said anything else. He waited until she was safely back inside.

She went back to her lab and grabbed a DNA swab. She knocked on the interrogation door. She put on her best tech face. "I'm here to get a DNA swab so we can exclude Mr. Stanich as our killer."

The man went white as a sheet. "I didn't kill anyone. I swear."

She uncapped it. "With your permission?"

"Yeah, yeah. Take it."

Freya swabbed his cheek and left. She had enough DNA to run a few tests. And she planned to get started. Now she needed a few more swabs. She made a phone call.

"Mr. Camhion, this is Freya Jensen. I'm wondering if I could get your help."

Eldridge's tone was tense. "I got a phone call from Ansel Reddick today. Claims you and Gideon accused him of murder."

Freya cleared her throat. "Gideon was not the most diplomatic. But there was cause to question him."

"He said Gideon found a deposit that matched the

ransom only a few days after Nash was found. He's been my friend for years. He wouldn't do this."

"As to that, I want to get some DNA from some of your friends, including Mr. Reddick. Right now, my best bet is process of elimination. We have the killer's DNA. If I can compare all your associates, I can exclude them and move on."

"I can see who can come by Camhion headquarters. Some won't, simply because of who they are."

Freya knew what he meant. Men with money. Many with secrets. "As to that, it would simply shine a light on them based on their refusal. Police might end up with a warrant to enforce it."

Eldridge chuckled. "I like your style, Ms. Jensen. I hear my son does, too. I'll set it up for tomorrow. You can come by my house tonight. My wife is out with friends, and Hayden and I are having drinks. You're welcome to ours."

"I'll call Nash to bring us."

* * *

Nash watched as Freya fussed with her clothes the second she stepped out of his car. "You look fine."

Freya yanked one last time and smoothed the wrinkles. "Easy for you to say. You always look like a million dollars."

He'd gotten used to the polo shirts with the MPD logo on them and her ill fitted slacks. He kissed her neck. "So do you."

The front door opened. "None of that now."

"Hi, Dad. Freya comes with swabs."

Nash saw her gawking. He grew up here, so to him, it was home. But he could tell she was taking in the artwork, the antiques, and the expensive damask drapes. "Come on."

Hayden rose from his chair. Nash was shocked at how frail he looked. It hadn't been that long since he'd seen him last. The man was fading fast. Doctors and lawyers. Can't die without a will, he supposed.

Freya wasn't apologetic as she swabbed first Eldridge then Hayden. "I appreciate your cooperation. It will be easy to eliminate you, Mr. Camhion. I already compared Nash's DNA to our killer's to be sure we didn't have Nash's DNA on file by mistake. I was happy to find they were not a match. A paternal match between you and Nash will, in turn, eliminate you."

"Glad to hear it. I can guarantee my DNA will match Nash." He smiled at her and gestured for her to sit.

Nash rested his hand on her thigh. Her tension was palpable. "How about you Hayden? DNA going to exclude you?"

Hayden's eyes narrowed. "Yes. I can guarantee that, too."

Nash clenched his teeth. "A man on his deathbed usually confesses."

"I'm not dead yet."

Freya glanced at Nash. He patted her thigh. "Good to hear."

Eldridge looked at his son. "Why don't you take your lady on a tour of the house and gardens. Cool off."

Nash did as he was told. He took Freya to the entryway. "Gardens are nice. My mother is an avid gardener. She has help, but they are lovely."

Freya followed him outside. Everything was in bloom. "Wow. Grandpa and I are terrible gardeners. Your mom, on the other hand, is amazing."

They were quiet for a while. They meandered through the garden. Nash spoke. "What is your impression of Hayden?"

Freya touched a bloom. "He's very sick. And you don't like him."

"You know why?"

She nodded. "I read about the embezzlement and scandal when I ran a full background check. And how he tried to drag your father's name through the mud."

Nash pulled her onto the garden bench. "Once a liar, always a liar. I never liked Hayden. Even as a kid. Gideon said you hadn't found anything that might tie him to the murder and kidnapping."

"No, I haven't."

Nash leaned back and stared up at the sky. "I used to sit out here a lot. Watched the clouds and tried to find shapes. Hayden is not the kidnapper."

"No."

"But he could have paid someone."

She nodded. "He could. I can confirm there was a lot more money going out than in, all those years ago. So many transactions it would be hard to tell if he was paying someone off. Things are still the same with him, financially speaking. If I had probable cause, Gideon could get a warrant. Or Donna. But it's just not there."

Nash had a feeling they were getting close. He wasn't

sure why, but something was nagging at him. "Speaking of Donna, how is she?"

"She's okay. Her partner has been keeping her up to date. He's the one who got the bank records. Gideon did the digging on our side. I do want to go see her if you don't mind."

Nash turned toward her. "I don't mind. We can stop by on the way home. I'm sorry about this morning. I don't mean to be a jerk. It just happens sometimes. I try hard to be in control. Of myself. Of my surroundings. And often those around me. Hence the prince moniker."

"It fits you. It's not hard to picture. But I'm no princess."

Nash took her hands in his. "Good. Because I don't want one. I want you, just as you are. I've been thinking that maybe it's not such a bad thing. You and me until death do us part."

Her mouth dropped open. "You're serious."

Nash laughed, his heart feeling light. "Yes. I can't promise the kid thing. But if you'll have me anyway, I want to marry you."

Freya's eyes dampened. "I love you, Nash. And yes."

Nash let out the breath he'd been holding. "Thank God. I don't have a ring. But I'll get one."

"What changed your mind?"

"Gideon, Trenton, and Isaac. I played cupid with two of them. I figure I'm pretty good at it. So it would make sense that I would find the perfect woman for me. And that I'd better snatch her up."

"And what about Gideon? Does he get extra credit?"

He knew she meant Gideon's art. "He gets credit for all

of us. Those portraits may be a coincidence, but they were a catalyst."

"So now what?"

Nash pulled her against his chest. "That's usually my line. I do have one concern. Grandpa Henry. How will he take it?"

She looked up at him. "Will we stay in D.C.?"

He didn't even have to think about it. "Yes."

"Then he'll be fine."

"I like him."

She hugged him. "Me, too. Your dad seems nice. A little annoyed with you, though."

"Pretty standard. I can be annoying. We should probably head out. We'll have to drop those swabs off and head to Donna's."

She rose. "Duty calls."

"Duty calls."

* * *

It had taken all her willpower to drop the samples off and not start processing them. She knew Nash was right. Tomorrow was soon enough. It was late when they got to Donna's. She knocked, but there was no answer. Concerned, Freya used her key.

Nash was right behind her. She stopped dead in her tracks. Donna was sitting at her kitchen table wearing a man's shirt. And the man across from her, sans the shirt, was her partner. She smiled at her best friend. "Well, well. Sorry, I'm interrupting."

Donna's face turned beet red. The man in the wheelchair shrugged. "At least I'm wearing pants. Gets mighty uncomfortable sitting on this thing naked."

Donna saw Nash behind Freya. "I should get dressed."

Nash was obviously suppressing a grin. "Not on my account."

Freya glanced back at him. "Anyway, I wanted to stop by to see how you were. And I have some DNA to process. And Brian, since you're here, Gideon is at the station right now trying to crack the tech that lost the DNA."

He nodded. "Warren Stanich. Fifty-seven. Teaches forensic seminars. Guy's a hack. I read your report. Hopefully Detective Eginhard will get him to talk. I assume you'll be back in the lab tomorrow with your DNA."

"Yes. I've also got Eldridge Camhion inviting some of his friends and colleagues to get DNA from them. Exclusionary, of course."

Brian smiled. "Of course. We're making progress. More than there's been in years. Call me if you find something."

Donna pouted. "I can't wait until I'm off leave. It's driving me crazy being stuck here. I want to help."

Brian turned to her. "Really? Nothing good came of it?"

She blushed. "Well, something really good came of it. And you might need to do it again to keep my mind off work."

Freya took a step back. "This is where we exit. Nash and I are going back to his house. We're planning a wedding."

Donna's mouth dropped open, much like hers had. "What?"

Nash stayed silent, though Freya could sense his

amusement. "I'll catch you up when you're done playing with Brian. I'll call you."

"You better."

Freya locked the door behind them. "That certainly wasn't what I was expecting. But I'm glad."

"Love is in the air."

Freya could only second that.

Chapter Thirteen

The week passed quickly. Freya knew she was pushing herself to her limits, but she was determined to crack this case. She didn't want to go into married life with this hanging over Nash's head. Assuming she and Nash got there.

They didn't discuss the proposal but fell into a routine of sorts. They made a second trip to pick up some more of her things, and they'd told Henry, but otherwise, their relationship was going much as it had before he proposed to her.

The computer dinged. Finally. She read the results, compared them, then checked again. It made an odd sort of sense. Nash did say he never liked him.

Freya sent Gideon a note and sent Brian a copy. She looked at her watch. Nash was in conference calls this morning. Cantwell was exceeding expectations, and Nash wanted to meet with the developers. He said he and Lilah would be in meetings until later in the day. Gideon was out; he had stopped by to check on her progress before he left.

Glancing at the clock and now impatient, she grabbed her purse and keys after sending everything to Brian and Gideon. Nash's house was less than half an hour from here. It was broad daylight. No one knew where she was headed.

She waved at a few people as she headed for her car.

Thankfully Grandpa Henry and his friend had dropped it off so it could sit outside the police station instead of outside his house. The lot was full of people. Some officers and staff. Some people there were desperate for help. Others belligerent and being dragged in for something they swore they were not guilty of. Freya had lost count of how many people had sworn up and down they were innocent, only to have forensic evidence say otherwise. But it also felt good when she could prove innocence; it kept her faith in humanity.

It was raining today, but she didn't mind. She navigated her way out of the clogged streets of downtown as she headed into the expensive neighborhood where Nash made his home.

She came to a stop. She saw a large van barreling down the road, going much faster than traffic allowed. She stayed at the stop sign, waiting for the van to blast through the intersection. But in a moment, she screamed as the van veered and collided with the driver's side of her car.

* * *

Nash's phone buzzed next to him. He glanced at the clock on the kitchen wall. Too early for Freya, so he ignored it. He smiled in satisfaction as he ran the numbers. Cantwell was making the quartet a small fortune. They hadn't broken even yet with the amount they'd invested, but they were getting closer. First quarter was all the proof he needed that they were a success.

Rubbing his eyes, he heard his front door slam. He stood

up and rushed to the living room. "Dad. What are you doing here?"

Eldridge tossed Nash his phone. "It's happening again."

Nash felt all the blood drain from his face. On the screen was a ransom demand. A quarter of a million dollars for her safe return. Her? "Where's Penny?"

Eldridge tried to catch his breath. "She's across the street trying to get a hold of Gideon. She didn't answer her phone. I tried to call you, but yours went to voicemail."

Nash felt his heart skip a beat. "If not Penny, who?"

Nash ran to his phone. There was no ransom demand on his phone. There was one missed call from his dad. And one from Freya. She never left him a voicemail, but there it was.

A sickly familiar voice came over the line. "Wasn't quite how I planned it; I admit. But I couldn't resist. How is your dad? Oh, I don't plan to touch a hair on Penny's pretty head. Not my type. You for her, Nash. No cops. Gideon better stay gone this time. I'll be waiting for your call."

Nash started to dial Freya's phone when his father pulled it from him. "Think, Nash. You can't face this guy alone. You don't even know who he is. If you go rushing to Freya, you'll both end up dead. And you know it. He won't let her go."

Nash felt panic rising but tamped it down. He needed his mind clear. For Freya. "The station. Try Gideon again. But the clock is ticking. There's no telling what he'll do to her."

Nash let his dad drive. Gideon's phone kept going to voicemail. "Damn it, Gideon. Answer me."

Eldridge broke a few traffic laws crossing town. They both rushed inside. Captain Barnes happened to be in the bullpen.

"Mr. Camhion. What are you doing here? We haven't called you yet."

Eldridge glanced at Nash. "Me or him?"

"You. Gideon just brought Hayden Brooks into custody."

Eldridge didn't understand. "Hayden? Why? What does he have to do with Freya's kidnapping?"

Barnes was stunned. "Freya's what?"

Nash explained quickly. Captain Barnes went to find Gideon.

Eldridge held his son before he collapsed. "We'll find her. Gideon will find her. Just like he found you."

Gideon ran into the bullpen. "What about Freya? She's not in her lab. Her team hasn't seen her since before lunch."

Nash pulled up the voicemail while Eldridge assured him Penny was fine. She was on her way to her mother to explain what happened. He'd already gotten a text saying she was safely there.

Gideon swore. "Freya sent me an email, but I was out. She ran the latest batch of DNA, and she linked Hayden Brooks to Warren Stanich. He's Warren's biological father."

Eldridge glanced at Nash. "We thought he only had a daughter."

Gideon gestured for them to follow him to the interrogation room. "DNA doesn't lie. And Freya would have triple-checked before sending me that email. And the fact that the DNA from the case was lost by Hayden's son creates a whole new set of questions."

Gideon opened the door. "You've got visitors."

Hayden's face was pale and his hand trembled. "What are you doing here? Your crazy friend made me come down here. He's been yelling at me for hours."

Eldridge was going to talk, but Nash pushed him aside. "Hayden, you son of a bitch. He's got Freya. You're going to tell me who he is, or I'll beat it out of you."

Gideon crossed his arms over his chest. "I'll let him."

Hayden's frightened gaze flashed to Eldridge. "I would never hurt you or your family."

Gideon held Nash back when he would have lunged at him. "Let Eldridge talk."

Eldridge sat and faced Hayden. "We've known each other a long time. We're family. Why? Why would you do this?"

Hayden coughed, a deep sound in his chest. "I didn't do anything."

"We know Warren purposely lost the DNA. And he did it for you. For once in your miserable life, do the right thing. Tell the truth. Do you want to go to your deathbed with this hanging over you?"

Hayden stopped arguing, all defiance draining from him. "I paid him. I knew what he was. Warren, he just wanted to please his old man. They were both supposed to leave and never come back. When I saw the news about the boy killed last year, I knew who it was. I knew. So did my son. Warren threatened to expose me if I didn't pay him a hundred thousand. But Warren never knew who it was that took Nash, though he'd seen the man's face the day Warren drove the getaway car."

"Paid who? Why?" Eldridge's voice broke with tears.

"I knew it would break you. Cormac had suspicions. He confronted me but had no proof. He knew you wouldn't believe him without proof. I knew it had to be then. And I needed to get rid of your heir. Without them, you would have folded. Camhion Enterprises would have been no more. And I would have stepped in. Your faithful employee and friend. Your cousin, who could be trusted with the Camhion business. Brooks Investments would have gotten all your clients, and I would have gotten your real estate for a song."

"You killed my father and had my son tortured for money?" Eldridge yanked Hayden to his feet.

The man stumbled. "After Cormac was killed, I was sorry I had ever started it. I called him and told him he needed to let Nash go. I told him he could do whatever he wanted first, but he had to return him. When I found out what had happened, I was shocked. I thought he'd molest him, not torture him."

Nash stood beside his father. "And you could live with that?"

Hayden's eyes shot daggers at Nash. "I have hated you since you were born. The perfect prince. He could have lit you on fire, and I wouldn't have cared."

Gideon stepped in. "His name. Now."

"Gregory Reddick."

Eldridge dropped into a chair. "Ansel knew?"

Hayden's strength faded and he sat facing Eldridge. "No. Ansel was a patsy. Greg didn't care about the money. But he didn't want to risk it being traced to him. So he dumped it in his father's account. Greg knew you'd never suspect his dad. Warren assured the police captain and Detective Dashevsky that there was no evidence that the people surrounding you were involved. Dashevsky didn't care. Case closed. When I found out Greg was back in town and working for his father, I knew this was going to come to a head. Greg has been obsessed with your son since the day he got away. But up until last year, he held up his side of the bargain and disappeared. When he returned, Warren wasn't far behind."

Gideon sent a quick note to Agent Lorenzo and Captain Barnes. "Where is he?"

"Same place Nash was with him last. A dingy house on the wrong side of town. Blocks from the childhood home of Gideon Eginhard."

Gideon yanked Eldridge and Nash with him. "I need to get a team and get over there. Every minute Freya is with that bastard, the less likely we'll find her in one piece."

Nash stopped him, his eyes stormy. "He wants me. Use me."

Eldridge stayed silent, though his eyes were pleading with Gideon to deny the request.

Gideon shook his head at Eldridge. "I'll keep him safe and bring him home. Just like last time. Nash, let's go. We need a plan."

* * *

The smell was just as he remembered it. Garbage littered

the alleys. It was dark and there was no one outside. It was this time of night that he'd escaped a crazed killer. And here he was going back in.

The siding was vandalized, and crude words and gang symbols covered the faded surface. The windowpanes were just glass shards on the ground. The windows had been boarded, and a condemned sign sagged on the front door. It was hard to believe the building was still standing. The lot next door was vacant, the weeds overgrown, and it didn't look like anyone had set foot inside in twenty-seven years.

Nash grabbed the doorknob to the front door and the door opened with a loud creek. He was unarmed, but that didn't matter. Nash had dreamed of this. Dreamed of finding the man who had done this and beating him until he begged for mercy.

He took out a flashlight. Nash scanned the dingy room, but there was no one. Gideon was in his ear, talking calmly, telling him what to do.

"Just keep breathing, Nash. Remember your training. You can do this." Gideon's mantra came over the line.

Nash went further in. The room where it all began was at the end of the hall. The door was open, beckoning him further in. He could see an old padlock dangling from the latch that had kept him inside. He shone a light into the room as he slowly made his way into the small space. Faint light came through the boarded windows. His heart stopped beating for a moment when he saw Freya on a filthy mattress and tied to the bed in the middle of the room. The same four-poster bed he'd been tied to twenty-seven years ago.

"Don't rush in, Nash. Stay calm."

Calm. He took a shallow breath, the dirt and the mold threatening to choke him. "Aren't you going to face me?"

A soft voice came from the shadows behind the bed. Keys jangled. "I've waited so long for you."

For a moment, black panic washed over him at the sound of those keys. But then Nash saw the shadow shift, and the panic subsided. This was just a man, not the monster of his nightmares. "I'm not a little boy anymore."

The man came into the light of the flashlight, his face under a mask. Not the medical one Freya saw, but the same mask he'd worn years before. A knife glinted in his hand. Light reflected off the gold bands. "You were the best. The very best. The others were no comparison to you. Your face. Your body. Your smell. Your skin. Your beautiful, delicate skin."

Nash ignored Gideon in his ear. "You said me for her. Let her go."

The man ran the blade across Freya's cheek. "She's soft, too. Her skin cuts like silk."

Gideon's frantic "don't" rang in Nash's ear. Nash took a step forward. "But I'm the best."

Gregory ran the blade down Freya's body, moving to her hands. He cut one tie, then the other. He intentionally cut her skin as he did it. Nash watched blood trickle down her hand as she moaned and turned her head on the bed.

Nash took another step closer. "Now her feet."

The man took glee in making a production of it. Blood soaked into her sock. She moaned a little more, and her eyes flickered open.

Her eyes were glazed, but they latched onto his. "Nash?"

Nash held the flashlight on Gregory as he came closer to the bed. "It's me. You're going to go home."

Her head wobbled as he pulled her to her feet. "Home. You're home."

He kissed her brow and held her to him. "Take this flashlight and go down the hall. Go straight outside. Keep going and don't stop."

Freya's hand gripped the flashlight. Tears fell. "I'm not leaving you here with him."

Nash shoved her toward the door. "Go."

"Isn't that sweet." The man held the knife and pointed to the bed. "Your turn."

"Not on your life. I said I'd trade. I didn't say I'd make it easy." Nash kept his eyes on his prey.

"When I'm through with you, I'll find her. And your sister. Everyone you've ever loved."

Nash jumped back when the man swung the blade at his midsection. "You'll have to do better, Gregory. I'm not a scared little boy anymore."

The man roared at the use of his name and lunged at him. The man was quick, quicker than Nash expected. They went down to the floor. The man's breath was on his cheek. His stomach revolted at the scent of peppermint and tobacco on his breath. Nash's vision dimmed for a moment until he felt the knife slice his forearm. Gregory was laughing at him, trying to pin him down, but Nash broke his hold and managed to roll out of the way and to his feet.

Gregory ripped off his mask. "Let me guess. My old pal Hayden spilled his guts. He always was a coward."

Nash felt his arm go numb as blood dripped down his sleeve. "Your pal Hayden isn't going to live long enough to stand trial. But you are. You murdered my grandfather."

In a rage, Gregory lunged at him. Nash lunged back, ducking so that he hit the man's midsection, avoiding the knife. They were well matched, but Nash had years of pent-up anger and rage to fuel him. Nash's martial arts training kicked in. Years of muscle memory fighting with Gideon took hold. Nash barely felt the knife graze his cheek as he wrestled and pinned the older man to the floor.

Nash slammed his wrist against the floor until the knife fell from Gregory's grip. Nash then took his fist and slammed it dead center into Gregory's face. The face of his tormentor. The face of his childhood demon. But he was nothing more than a man, a pathetic man who preyed on those weaker than him.

Nash struck him again and felt his nose break. The man was laughing at him as blood dripped from his nose.

Nash's arm lifted for another swing but felt a strong grip on his arm before he could hit him again. He was yanked to his feet.

Gideon held him as another officer yanked Gregory Reddick to his feet. "I'd rather let you keep pounding on him, but I'm supposed to be one of the good guys. And so are you."

Nash sagged against him. "Freya?"

"She's with the paramedics. She was drugged. Likely the same drug he used on you and the other boys."

Nash gripped his arms. "He said he cut her."

Gideon waited until Gregory had been removed. "He

did, Nash. Some are bad. But she'll be fine. I don't think he meant to kill her."

Nash felt his knees weaken and leaned on Gideon as they left the house. He glanced back. "I hope this place burns."

They went to the paramedics. Freya was weakly fighting them. "I need to get to Nash. He's with him. He made me leave. I shouldn't have left."

Nash rushed to her side. "I'm right here, Freya. Right here. He's in custody. You're going to be fine."

She started to cry. It broke Nash's heart.

"We need to go." The paramedics started lifting the gurney.

Nash started to climb in. Gideon came over. "They found her car. The accident looked bad. It might not be drugs, Nash, that are making her so weak."

Gideon helped Nash into the ambulance and joined him. "Freya, can you tell me what happened?"

She turned her head, but her eyes stayed closed. "I was at a stop sign. Big van. Rammed me. He pulled me out. I couldn't fight him. I tried."

Nash's stomach clenched. There was blood seeping through her clothes across her stomach. And there was blood behind her head. The words from the paramedics were miles away. Gideon held onto Nash while Nash held Freya's hand and willed the ambulance to hurry.

* * *

Nash paced. He'd refused treatment until Gideon forced him to get seen. He had stitches on his arm, and the cut on his face cleaned. It was superficial. Wouldn't even leave a scar. "God, Gideon."

Gideon rose. He pulled Nash into his arms. "She'll be okay. You saved her. Hold onto that."

Isaac and Trenton stormed in. Ginny, Lilah, and Penny weren't far behind. The men immediately embraced their friends.

When they stepped back, Penny took their place. "Nash."

He hugged his sister to him, thankful she was fine. That she, too, hadn't been targeted. "I love you, Penny. More than you'll ever know."

Tears burned her eyes. "I love you more than you'll ever know. And I'm so proud of you. When you're feeling better, I'm going to punch you for making me worry."

He released her and kissed her knuckles. "Mom and Dad on their way?"

"Yeah. Mom wanted to wait for Dad to come get her, now that we know you're in one piece. She's going to box your ears for this stunt, Gideon too."

Gideon pulled Penny to him. "Nash deserved closure."

Penny glanced at Nash's swollen knuckles. "I would have loved to take a swing at him myself. I'm told he's at a different hospital."

Gideon glanced at the entrance as Eldridge and Victoria came in. "I didn't want him anywhere near our family."

Victoria rushed to her son. She kissed him and held him, her scent pouring over him. Then she pulled back. "Of all the foolish, stupid stunts you've pulled over the years, this takes the cake. What were you thinking? I'll tell you. You weren't thinking."

Nash smiled at her as she railed, one he couldn't suppress. "I love you, Mom."

She turned to Gideon and poked her tiny finger into his chest. "And you. You let him. Encouraged him, no doubt. He could have been killed. You both could have been killed. What if he had a gun? Huh? Then what would you have done?"

Eldridge took his wife into his arms as she started weeping. "You can yell at them later. How is Freya?"

Victoria got a grip. "How is she? Where is she?"

"I don't know. Her grandpa arrived shortly after we did. He kicked me out. Not that I blame him. I'm the reason she was taken. I haven't heard from either of them since."

The group took a seat. Nash stayed at the window, watching the moon as clouds passed by.

It was two hours before Henry appeared. He looked tired, but he looked relieved. "She's okay. They did some tests. She banged her head but doesn't look like a concussion. No internal injuries they can find. She's going to be kept and monitored. And you, young man, when this is over, you and I are having a long chat. But right now she wants to see you. Doctor is in with her now."

Nash nodded as guilt ate at him and headed back to where Henry had come from. His family would take care of him. Gideon would give him the full story. But right now, Nash just wanted to see Freya. He went to the room where the nurse directed him.

Freya's eyes brightened. "Nash."

He came to her side and took her hand. He leaned in and kissed her lightly.

Her gaze slid away. "This is Dr. Anderson."

The older woman shook his hand. Her dark hair was pulled back from her face as she read the chart. "Two of the five lacerations on her stomach needed stitches. She'll need help with the three on her back to keep them clean. Only one needed stitches. Cuts on her hands and feet are minor. Thankfully the injuries she sustained during the car accident were minimal. Due to her condition, we had to do an MRI, but the scan was normal. There was a sedative found in her system, but it shouldn't have hurt the fetus."

Nash pulled away. "The what?"

Freya tried to sit up but gave up when her arms wouldn't support her. "Nine weeks, Nash. To the day."

Nash swallowed. Then he did the last thing anyone would have expected of him. He laughed. He laughed until his eyes watered.

Freya managed to sit up this time. "Do you need a sedative? I didn't expect hysterics."

He came to her side and pulled her into his arms. "Fate certainly has enjoyed playing games with me my entire life."

Freya pulled away. "I know. I'm sorry, but..."

He stopped her. "But this is one game I am going to enjoy playing."

* * *

Freya couldn't be convinced to stay home. Henry had yelled, half in English and half in Norwegian. He'd let Nash try to convince her, but he'd had no luck. Gideon hadn't helped. He wanted every 't' crossed and every 'i' dotted. He needed Freya to be the one to do it. Freya's only concession was to keep her work hours to a minimum and to eat three meals a day.

He had been worried about Freya. The first few nights she woke in the throes of a nightmare. Nash had barely slept, and he'd been there to hold her when she woke. But as the reality of her pregnancy started making itself known, the fear of her kidnapping started to fade. She claimed she was too dizzy and too nauseous to worry about Gregory Reddick. She said he wasn't worth the effort.

He knew she was more worried about him than herself. She was worried he was hiding his true feelings about the pregnancy. He'd done what he could to convince her otherwise. But he wasn't upset. In the quiet moments at the hospital, while Freya slept and he was alone with his thoughts, he'd come to terms with the fact that he would be a father. The legacy his grandfather wanted would be fulfilled. With that thought, and the knowledge that the man responsible for murdering his grandfather was behind bars, peace filled some of the darker spots inside him where peace hadn't been before. He knew the darkness wouldn't completely fade, but he took Isaac's words to heart. He would do whatever he had to do to protect Freya and his family.

It took two weeks to finish collecting the evidence. She'd refused to answer any of Nash's questions. Gideon also kept his mouth closed. The FBI lab, along with Donna and Brian, was also working double time, putting the last of the nails in Gregory's coffin. The Feds were bringing twelve counts of murder and thirteen counts of kidnapping against him. MPD was bringing the murder of Cormac Camhion to trial, as well as Freya's kidnapping and assault.

Nash closed his computer down as he heard voices downstairs. Lilah followed him.

Isaac waved at him, but his eyes went to his wife. "Hey, Nash. We heard the news about Hayden pleading guilty. Gideon called and said the last of the evidence against Gregory was turned over today."

Nash waved them all in. He'd heard that morning Hayden pleaded guilty to all charges. What little time he had left would be spent in prison.

"His son, Warren, took a plea deal. He's been spilling his guts for a lesser sentence. Claims all he did was tamper with evidence. In the end, Hayden didn't have much of a choice. He'd already confessed and taking it to trial would delay the inevitable. He's going to spend the rest of his life in jail either way. It makes the case against Gregory Reddick that much stronger."

Trenton and Ginny closed the door behind them. Ginny kissed Nash's cheek. "I hope he rots there for a long time."

Trenton squeezed her hand when Ginny came back to his side. "Don't we all. Death is too easy."

Nash smiled at his friends. "Where's Penny?"

The door opened. "I'm here. Gideon said he's on his way home. I told him he and Freya weren't going to be allowed to dodge our questions anymore."

Eldridge and Victoria arrived a little while later with food. "We brought dinner."

Nash let his mom fuss in his kitchen. He took a seat beside his dad. "How are you doing?"

Eldridge patted his son's hand. "Still so hard to believe. But the Camhions are strong. We survived before. We'll survive this."

Penny chimed in. "Thrive."

Eldridge smiled at his daughter. "Thrive."

Freya and Gideon came in an hour later. They both had the same look of satisfaction.

Freya came and took the seat Eldridge vacated. She gave him a small smile. "Thanks. I'm exhausted. And starving."

Nash pulled her legs across his lap. "Mom's getting food ready."

Victoria brought Freya the first plate. "Eat up, dear."

Gideon stood near the windows. "Gregory Reddick is pleading guilty to all charges."

Nash's hands tightened on Freya's legs. "All of them?"

Gideon turned to him. "All but one. He is refusing to plead guilty to your attempted murder. He claims he wasn't going to kill you the night you were rescued. He claims he wanted to keep you, and that's why he was moving you. He refuses to say where, just that it's a special place."

Freya slowly shook her head. "I'll find it."

Nash brushed her bangs back. "I have no doubt."

Eldridge's voice was hoarse. "But otherwise, he pleaded guilty to the rest? My dad's murder? The murder of the other twelve boys?"

Freya spoke around the food in her mouth. "All. Not that he had much choice between Hayden and Warren. I found where he bought the knife. He bought it from a collector years ago. I found some old receipts along with his knife collection. Trace DNA found on the knife he had on him during his arrest matched his last victim. The boy's mother broke down in tears when Gideon told her. But she's happy we found him. Maybe she'll sleep a little easier. His dad and sister, too."

Gideon scrubbed the fatigue from his eyes. "Greg Reddick has been watching you for a long time, Nash. There were hundreds of photos on his computer going all the way back to just after your kidnapping. Most recent photos included images of Donna, Freya, and me. He hired a private investigator who discovered who Donna was. He had images of her when she flashed her badge. Captain got a warrant and is having the PI's records confiscated. Greg also knows I've been investigating Cormac's murder. Hayden told him. Nash, I should have let you pound on him, too. Ever since Warren and Greg came back to town, Hayden has been keeping his eyes and ears open. It's why he's been working at Camhion and trying to get on everyone's good side. After Clara tried to kill Penny, and he was interrogated, Hayden claims it wasn't a stretch to realize I would be investigating Cormac's murder and Nash's kidnapping. He knew he needed to stay close."

Eldridge wiped the tears he was visibly trying to hold in. "I should have listened to you, Nash. I wanted to believe he'd changed. That he meant it when he said he wanted to make amends."

Nash conceded. "Part of him did want to make amends. The other part of him wanted to see how close the cops were coming to the truth. And he knew his DNA wasn't going to tie back to the murder. But he never thought we'd tie him to the forensic analyst who hid the DNA sample for him all those years ago."

Freya waved her fork at Nash. "Genetic genealogy worked on this case, just not how we planned."

Eldridge got control of himself. "I haven't heard from Ansel. He only spoke to me once. He told me he hired Gregory a lawyer but would fully cooperate with the investigation. Doubt we'll hear from him again. The only thing left is for the judge to sentence Gregory to life in prison."

Victoria stood up. "It's over. I don't want to ever hear that man's name again. Let's eat."

And then...

The party was in full swing. Nash's fortieth birthday party was a hit. Of course, he mused, it would have had a better wine selection had he planned it. But Isaac planned the menu, cooked it with Lilah's help, and the food was amazing. Freya had already had two platefuls. They were having the party at Isaac's home. Nash considered it the birthplace of Cantwell, and there was no other place he'd rather have his party than here, surrounded by his friends and family.

"Enjoying yourself, Mrs. Camhion?"

Freya swallowed her bite. "I'm having a lovely time, Ignatius. Remind me to invite us to Isaac's house for dinner more often."

Nash handed her the glass of sparkling water he'd grabbed for her. "Have I told you how beautiful you look tonight?"

She set a hand on her stomach. "You mentioned it a time or two. You do seem to like the dress. You did make me wear it to our wedding. I figured I'd better wear it one last time while it still mostly fits."

Nash laid a hand over hers. "And when we get home, I'm going to enjoy getting you out of it."

Gideon swung over. "I need to steal the birthday boy for a minute."

Freya waved them off. "I'm going to go chat up the ladies. Donna is chatting with Penny, Ginny, and Lilah. I'm going to snag your mother on the way. Grandpa Henry, Brian, and Eldridge are off admiring Isaac's book collection. Come find me when you're done talking about whatever manly stuff it is you guys talk about."

Nash followed Gideon. "All good things, I hope."

Gideon smiled. "All good things. No bad things allowed, remember? We made a pact."

Nash had teased over a year ago that they needed to make a pact. This time he made them make one. "So what sort of surprise have you guys come up with?"

Trenton waved them over. "I do love a good exploding present. But Isaac was worried your heart couldn't take it."

Isaac nudged him. "It's his birthday. And he's had a rough couple of months. Cut him some slack."

Trenton's brow rose. "Yes, sir. Keep that up, and we'll be calling you prince."

Gideon hushed them. "That title is going to be passed on soon. Freya said the baby is a boy."

Nash shrugged. "Next time I'll try harder for a girl. But frankly, I'll be relieved when Ignatius Junior arrives. In truth, I'm not sure my heart can take it. Freya puked all over the bathroom this morning. You should have heard the cuss words coming out of her mouth. You've not heard a woman cuss until you've heard one swear at you in Norwegian."

Gideon shuddered. Then he straightened. "It feels right. To have you be the first. Penny's pregnant. Probably a month or so behind Freya. Penny wanted me to be the one to tell you. Our babies will grow up together."

Nash felt his eyes fill as congratulations were passed around. His baby sister was having a baby. "It does feel right, doesn't it? We'll have to take bets who's next. Lilah or Ginny."

Trenton glanced around the corner. "Hundred bucks on Ginny."

Isaac's brows rose. "Two on Delilah."

Gideon considered it. "I don't know. I think my money is on Isaac. He's the studious type. He'll figure out the fastest, most efficient way to get Delilah pregnant to collect that bet."

Nash slapped his hand on Trenton's arm. "My money is on my pal Trenton. He's like the little engine that could."

Nash's stomach hurt once the group stopped laughing. "You do know Lilah and Ginny will kill us for this, right?"

Isaac shrugged, his tone pragmatic. "If anyone is going to do me in, I'd rather it be Delilah."

Trenton smiled. "A man can only hope. I know how Ginny would do me in."

Gideon finally got the group under control. "Anyway, tonight is about Nash. And Ignatius Junior. Though I really hope you find a new name for that baby before he's born."

Nash shook his head. "Nope. Freya is insistent. She wanted to honor my grandfather's memory. And she's fond of my name. Ignatius after my grandfather, and Liam after Freya's father."

Gideon considered it. "Ignatius Liam Camhion. Nice strong name."

Trenton seconded it. "I assume he'll be Liam."

Nash took a sip of his wine. "Got that right."

Freya came up behind him. "I told you; I love the name Ignatius. And I love you."

Nash turned his back on his friends. He kissed her lingeringly, his hand caressing her stomach, while the quartet pretended not to watch. He turned back to his friends. "So, where's my present?"

Gideon set out a box. "The framed game art is from Lilah. The crystal dragon is from me and Penny, and the crib mobile is from Isaac."

Isaac interjected. "All from Norwegian mythology, I might add."

Trenton continued. "The treasury bonds are from me and Ginny. Can never start too early investing in the kid's future. And the pendant is from all of us."

The gifts were so thoughtful that he felt himself choking up again. Freya was examining the rest of the gifts.

Gideon handed him a box that was set to the side. "The Cantwell Quartet."

Nash took out the gold pendant. It was the symbol Gideon drew for Cantwell. His finger caressed the shining metal. "Unity, friendship, strength, and love."

Gideon nodded. "Unbreakable."

Nash held out his hands. The others joined. The men formed a circle. Unity of the four. "Unbreakable."

From The Author

The Prince. I wanted Nash to get justice. There is so much pain inside him from all that he endured throughout his life. He was afraid to grab ahold of life with both hands. And to hold a woman in his heart.

If you read my "From The Author" section in the previous three books, you'll remember the characters are based on characters in a video game. Nash is based on a prince. During the story of the game, the woman he is to marry is murdered. It's interesting how the game writers brought them together at the end. Not sure if they're both ghosts, or if it's a dream, but it's sweet to see them reunited.

In my story, Nash comes full circle, and he lives happily ever after. The key to Nash's story was that it had to end where it all began.

About the series: The Cantwell Quartet is centered around four men: the prince, the protector, the peacemaker, and the comedian. Not sure that is how the game writers thought of them, but that's how I do. The four men fight side by side to save the kingdom, and ultimately, the world. Each has flaws. Each has secrets and pain. And each of them does what's right. My kind of heroes!

I hesitate to name the game for two reasons. One, the books are not based on the storylines in the game, so I don't want to disappoint fans who think they're getting fan fiction, or a modern-day book version of the game. The books are my stories with my interpretation of who these men could be in modern day. And two, it's more fun to keep you guessing. But if you guess right, I'll tell you.

Also, if you enjoyed this book, or any of my other titles, please consider leaving a rating at your favorite retailer, Goodreads and/or Bookbub. And if you have the time, a text review would be lovely. Indie authors rely on readers like you to tell others how much you enjoy their books.

Happy reading,